Murder
A Freshly Baked Cozy Mystery
by
Kate Bell
Kathleen Suzette

Books by Kathleen Suzette:

A Rainey Daye Cozy Mystery Series

Pumpkin Spice Donuts and a Murder
A Rainey Daye Cozy Mystery, book 14

A Pumpkin Hollow Mystery Series
Candy Coated Murder
A Pumpkin Hollow Mystery, book 1
Murderously Sweet
A Pumpkin Hollow Mystery, book 2
Chocolate Covered Murder
A Pumpkin Hollow Mystery, book 3
Death and Sweets
A Pumpkin Hollow Mystery, book 4
Sugared Demise
A Pumpkin Hollow Mystery, book 5
Confectionately Dead
A Pumpkin Hollow Mystery, book 6
Hard Candy and a Killer
A Pumpkin Hollow Mystery, book 7
Candy Kisses and a Killer
A Pumpkin Hollow Mystery, book 8
Terminal Taffy
A Pumpkin Hollow Mystery, book 9
Fudgy Fatality
A Pumpkin Hollow Mystery, book 10
Truffled Murder
A Pumpkin Hollow Mystery, book 11
Caramel Murder
A Pumpkin Hollow Mystery, book 12
Peppermint Fudge Killer
A Pumpkin Hollow Mystery, book 13

Table of Contents

Chapter One

IT HAD NEVER FELT SO good to be home. I had enjoyed spending Christmas with my mother in my hometown of Goose Bay, Alabama, but my daughter Jennifer and I had come too close to becoming murder victims. Now that a new year was here, I had made up my mind that it was going to be a good one. I had a new love in my life, and I was working on a new career, even if I hadn't pinned down all the details yet.

The sun was shining down on Alec and me as we ran through my neighborhood. In spite of the early morning cold, I could tell it was going to be a warm day. Warm for January in Maine, at least.

I took a swig from my water bottle, and we crossed the street and headed for my house. The closer we got to the marathon we planned to run in May, the less prepared I felt. I still had an extra five pounds I needed to lose after spending Christmas with my mother. Darn those fresh buttermilk biscuits slathered in butter and homemade strawberry jam. But a girl has gotta do what a girl has gotta do, and now I was paying the price.

"I have the best idea ever," Alec said, as we finished our run and headed inside my house.

"Do tell," I said and took a seat on the bench located along a wall inside my mudroom. I grabbed my everyday shoes from under the bench and began untying my running shoes. After a few weeks of treadmill running and staring at a blank wall, I had paid extra for a pair of shoes that would help stay me on my feet on icy and snowy roads and sidewalks. I had missed running outside.

"Let's make snow cream," he said. "I haven't made it in a couple of years."

"Snow cream? Thaddeus used to make that. But it's sunny out, and the weather channel said there wouldn't be any new snow for a couple of days," I pointed out. Thaddeus was my late husband, and he had loved the outdoors.

He shrugged. "So? It snowed last night."

He was right. It *had* snowed the previous evening, but we hadn't thought ahead to put a bowl out to catch clean snow. "We missed the snow," I said. "We can watch and put a bowl out when it gets ready to snow again."

"Why?" he asked. He had his right foot on the bench, tying his shoe.

"Because we want clean snow? If we're going to eat it, right?" I wasn't sure why he wasn't making the connection.

He chuckled. "We'll get clean snow. We're going to drive out to the woods and find some fresh, clean snow. We'll fill up a bucket and make a big bowl of snow cream."

"Uh, wait a minute," I said. "You're going to get the snow off the ground? And eat it?" He had to be out of his mind. Who did that? I wanted my snow to be guaranteed clean, without any critters having made tracks, or worse, through it.

"That's right, smarty pants. Right off the ground. It tastes better that way. Back to nature and all that."

"Says you. What if Yogi Bear, you know, did his business in it?" I asked, raising an eyebrow at him. Surely he had thought of that, right?

He laughed and put his foot back on the floor. "I'm pretty sure we'll be able to tell if Yogi has been anywhere near the snow we're going to get. I promise you, we'll get clean snow. I've been doing this all my life, and I know what I'm doing."

I sighed. "Well, I guess if you know what you're doing. But let's get some breakfast first. I'm starving."

I wasn't at all sure he knew what he was talking about. Everyone I knew that went to the trouble of making snow cream simply left a large bowl or bucket outside when it was snowing and collected what they needed. Sure, I'd heard of people going out to the woods to get snow, but I figured all those people must be doomsday preppers or whatever it was they were calling themselves these days.

I quickly scrambled up some eggs, and Alec made toast and coffee. Nothing fancy, but it was warm and filling. There was something about the smell of coffee on a winter morning that made me happy. It also made me feel warm and cozy, and I wondered if it was too early in the morning for a nap. I had flannel sheets on my bed, and the long run had worn me out. A nap sounded good.

"Hey," Jennifer said sleepily as she wandered into the kitchen and stretched. She wore flannel pajamas and white fluffy bunny slippers. Her tattered Hello Kitty bathrobe was wrapped loosely around her body.

"Good morning, Jennifer," Alec said. His dark hair was mussed after our run, but he was still handsome as ever.

Jennifer hadn't been crazy when Alec first made an appearance in our lives, but ever since our we-almost-got-murdered scare last month, she had been nicer to Alec. I didn't raise any fool. She knew Alec had a gun and that he knew how to use it. That sort of thing could come in handy in an emergency, and it had when a crazed murderer had taken both of us hostage.

"There are more scrambled eggs in the skillet, but you'll have to make your own toast," I said.

"And guess what we're doing?" Alec asked her, sounding like a kid on Christmas morning.

"What?" she asked, stumbling to the coffee maker and pouring herself a cup.

"We're going out to the woods to collect some snow and make snow cream," he said happily.

She turned and looked at him with an arched brow. "Why are you going out to the woods?"

"He likes his snow wild-caught. It has a different bouquet than domesticated snow," I supplied.

"Yeah, I bet it has a different bouquet. Eau de deer pee," she said.

I snickered. Like mother, like daughter.

Alec sighed. "You two are not very adventurous. You need to step out of your comfort zones. I assure you, other people make snow cream this way and live to tell the tale."

"Yes, people who live in tents and don't have access to electricity," I said.

Alec gave me the stink eye, and I smiled big at him. We finished up our breakfast and got ready to leave.

"You sure you don't want to come along, Jennifer?" Alec asked as we headed out the door.

"Nope. I'm good. Thanks," she said, slumping over her cup of coffee at the kitchen table, phone in hand. Jennifer had never been a morning person.

Alec's black SUV had belonged to the police department, and when he retired on December 31st, it had gone back. He was on foot until he could find a car he liked. I let him drive my car since he was sure he knew exactly where to get clean snow. We left town behind us, and after fifteen minutes of driving out into nowhere, I was starting to get worried. Just where was this clean snow?

"Hey, where are we going?" I finally asked him. "We've been driving a long time."

He smiled. "You're such a worrywart," he said and pulled off the road. "We'll walk into the woods a little way, and there will be miles and miles of clean snow."

"Okay, if you're sure about that," I mumbled and got out of the car, pulling my coat closer. A breeze had kicked up, and I wondered if I was wrong about it being a warm day or if the weather was just somehow colder out in the wild.

Alec reached into the backseat of my car and pulled out the two white buckets and two small shovels we had brought. The buckets had originally held ice cream and were two and a half gallons each. I wondered if we needed that much snow. It seemed like overkill.

"Come on," he said, taking my gloved hand.

The snow along the side of the road had been plowed, and the area was smooth, but as we got closer to the edge of the woods, I realized I'd made a mistake in not putting boots on. My feet were already wet and cold, and we hadn't even walked through deep snow yet.

"I'm not wearing appropriate shoes for this," I said.

"I know, but it will only take us a few minutes. I promise," he said. "We'll turn the heater on high on the way back."

We walked into the woods, and the snow was surprisingly still light and fluffy. I looked at it, wondering how many animals had tread through it, but I didn't see any obvious signs. Maybe Alec did know what he was talking about.

"How much further?" I asked, as my breath left my mouth in puffs of white clouds.

"Just over here, I think," he said. "We want to try and scoop up the top layer as much as possible, otherwise our snow cream will be filled with hard ice."

"Okay," I said. "What about over there?" I saw a mound of snow, and it looked pristine. I was sure no animal had gone anywhere near it.

"That looks good. You start over there, and I'll start right over here," he said, indicating a smaller mound on his left.

"Are we going to fill up both buckets?" I asked, heading to the larger mound I had spotted.

"Yeah, mound them up, too. Some of it will melt on the way home. We can put the buckets in the trunk so it'll stay colder."

I stopped in front of the mound and examined it, then walked slowly around it. I bent over and stuck my finger in it. It looked clean beneath the surface. I stood up straight and appraised it. It looked as clean as could be, and I decided it would pass muster.

Using my small shovel, I scooped up a layer of snow and put it in the bucket. I scooped a second time and hit something solid. *That's odd.* I tried another spot and scooped some off the top and put it in the bucket, and then tried again in another place and hit something hard again. I tried a few more spots and kept hitting something solid after the first scoop. I glanced over at Alec who seemed to be scooping away at the light, fluffy snow and getting his bucket filled nicely. *Huh. This might be harder than I thought.*

Chapter Two

I SCOOPED UP SOME MORE snow and put it in my bucket and then went for another scoop and hit something solid again. Figuring the mound must be a fallen tree covered in snow, I moved over to the other end and tried again. The first scoop of snow came easily, but the second hit the solid thing.

I leaned over and peered at the mound and saw something pink. *What is that?* I scraped the snow away from the pink area and realized it was a fabric of some kind. I couldn't imagine what pink fabric would be doing on a fallen tree trunk, so I scraped some more. The pink led to something blue, and I realized it looked like a knit scarf. I scraped some more, and when I saw blue-tinged lips; I screamed for all I was worth and stumbled backward until I fell on my backside. I screamed some more and scrambled to right myself and get on my feet.

"What is it?" I heard Alec call.

"Oh, oh, oh," I said, dancing around in a circle once I got up. "Alec!"

Alec was at my side before I could finish saying his name. "What is it? What's going on?"

I pointed at the mound. "Oh no, oh no, oh no," I said, trying not to look at it, but not able to keep from doing so.

Alec stepped in closer and then kneeled and brushed some snow away. "Wow."

Without another word, he took his cell phone from his pocket and dialed. "George, this is Alec Blanchard. Allie and I are out in the woods. We found a body," he said. He gave George the particulars on how to find us and pressed end on his phone.

"This is horrible," I said, feeling on the verge of tears. "It's a woman, isn't it?" That much I had seen.

He nodded, squatting next to the body again. He took his phone out and took some pictures. Then he carefully wiped snow away from the area I had seen the lips. "Do you recognize her?" he asked me after a couple of minutes.

"I don't know, I looked really fast," I said. I took a couple of steps closer, but I didn't want to look.

Alec began silently taking more pictures with his phone from different angles. Then he stepped back and took some of the surrounding areas. When he was done, he brushed more snow from her face and neck. She was wearing a pink coat with a baby blue scarf. He took more pictures of her.

I took a couple of steps closer and leaned over. "Oh my gosh, I do know who that is."

"Who?" Alec asked, looking up at me.

"Iris Rose," I said.

"Sounds like a hippie name?" he asked, looking at me quizzically.

"No, she's a second grade teacher at Belmont Elementary. She's kind of blue in the face, but I'm pretty sure that's her.

She was Jennifer's second grade teacher. It was her first year of teaching. Jennifer just loved her." I was suddenly sad. Iris had been fresh out of college and starry-eyed at the idea of making a difference in a room full of second-graders' lives.

Alec shook his head. "That's a shame."

"I wonder what happened to her? Can you tell?" I asked, taking another step forward. Iris's pale blue eyes stared sightlessly up at the mid-morning sky. I shivered and looked away.

"No, I don't want to uncover any more of her without the police getting here and taking a look," he said and then chuckled. "It sounds kind of nice saying—the police—and not meaning myself."

"I guess it would," I said. "I think retiring was a smart move."

"I do too," he said and stood up. "There's not much else we can do besides wait. The fresh snow that fell last night covered any footprints there might have been. I don't remember there being any tire tracks in the area where we parked."

As we stood there, dark clouds gathered overhead and blocked out the sun. I looked up. "Do you think it's going to snow again?"

"Could be," he said, looking up at the sky.

It was getting colder, and I wanted to go home. It seemed like it was taking George a long time to get here, and I just wanted to distance myself from Iris's body.

"Do you think she was murdered?" I asked him after a few minutes.

He looked at me. "Allie, did you think she walked out here and committed suicide by laying down and freezing to death?"

I sighed loudly. "No, Alec, I guess not." *Smartypants.*

"Oh, did you want to put your snow in the trunk of the car?" he asked, eyeing the bucket I still held in my hand. I had somehow managed to keep hold of the bucket when I hit the ground.

I narrowed my eyes at him. "We are not making snow cream from the snow that was on a dead body, do you understand me?" I dropped the bucket where I stood.

He just laughed at me.

"WOW, YOU KNOW WHO THAT looks like?" George Feeney asked Alec.

"Iris Rose?" Alec answered.

George nodded. "That's right. She was a real nice lady."

"All my kids had her in second grade and loved her," Yancey Tucker said, shaking his head.

Yancey, George, and three other police officers had shown up after twenty minutes, and the coroner was on his way. It was only the fifth of January, and the year wasn't starting as bright as I had anticipated.

The police took more pictures of the body and the area and then began scraping snow away. Iris was good and frozen. I felt heartsick and tried to remember if she had any children. I hoped that if she did, they were grown. Not that it would change the fact that they would grieve, but somehow in my mind, it made it easier if they were grown.

Alec bent down and touched her jacket. "That Jacket isn't ideal for being out here in the woods. It's not very heavy, and it isn't zipped."

I peered over his shoulder. "She has a scarf and knit cap. Maybe that makes up for it."

"Maybe. But if I were going to be out in the woods in the snow, I'd wear something heavier. Especially since the past four or five days have been windy and snowing, and frigidly cold," he said, as he removed the snow from around her body. "She doesn't have gloves on."

"Yeah, you're right. She isn't dressed for cold weather," I agreed. Iris's poor fingers had turned blue and the plain gold wedding band she wore glinted in the sunlight. As we stood there, light snow began to fall.

"We'd better get this done," George said.

George and Yancey worked to remove the remaining snow from her body and I saw she was wearing jeans. Those wouldn't be very warm either unless she was wearing thermals underneath.

"She's a tiny thing, too. You'd think she'd get cold easily," Yancey said.

"Can you tell how she died?" I asked. I couldn't see any blood from where I stood.

"Nothing obvious," Alec said. "We might not know the cause of death until the medical examiner does his job."

I nodded. I was stumped on who would do such a thing to Iris. I had never heard a negative thing said about her.

"She's laying very straight, with her hands folded over her stomach," Alec noted.

"Almost like she was laying in a coffin," George said.

"Exactly," Alec agreed and kneeled beside her. "And there's something in her hand."

"What?" George asked.

Alec stuck his finger near Iris's thumb and index finger and worked it under her hand. "I don't know. Her hands are too frozen to move."

The chief of police, Sam Bailey, showed up, and the guys got him caught up on what they knew so far. Alec hadn't really gotten along with Sam when he worked for him, but he always behaved as if it didn't bother him. I was pretty sure that was just an act.

Sam sighed. "Alec, what do you say you help us out with this investigation?"

Alec jerked his head up to look at him. "Sure," he said, nodding. It surprised me that Sam would ask, but Alec was his usual cool self about it.

Alec was working on getting his PI license but was nowhere near done with the requirements. He must have been as shocked as I was to hear Sam ask for his help.

"I'd appreciate it. With you retiring and Mills transferring out, we're a little shorthanded," Sam said.

"No problem." Alec looked him in the eye. "I can do that."

I wanted to stick my tongue out at Sam. The big jerk. If he'd treated Alec a little nicer when he worked for him, he might not have retired as early as he had. Alec still hadn't gone into any detail about what the issue was with Sam, but it was obvious to me Sam didn't like him much.

We stayed until the coroner arrived and he had been briefed. The snow was really starting to come down by that time, making everyone's job harder.

"Let's go. There isn't anything else we can do here," Alec said and took my hand.

My feet were soaked and frozen, and I was more than ready to head home. All I wanted was to soak my feet in some warm water and build a fire in the fireplace.

"What do you think about it?" I asked him as we headed to the car.

"I don't know. Like I said, I didn't see any obvious signs of trauma. We may not know how she died for a while," he said, as we got into the car.

When Alec started the car, I turned the heat on full blast and groaned. "That feels so good."

"Now we're going to have to wait to make snow cream another time," he said.

"I tell you what. I'll just set a bucket out to catch the snow when we get home. That will make the most perfect snow cream you've ever tasted," I said.

"You just don't know how to live," he said, pulling onto the highway.

I sighed. "I just cannot get it out of my mind. Who would have done that to Iris? She was so sweet. All the kids loved her."

"That's a shame, for sure," he said. "Was she married?"

I nodded. "Yes, but I can't remember if she had any children. When Jennifer was in her class, she was still young and had just gotten married. Her husband is a teacher too, if I remember right. Over at the high school."

"First stop tomorrow is to pay her husband a visit," he said.

"Who's going to tell her husband that she's dead?" I asked him.

"Sam will probably have George or Yancey go talk to him. They'll ask him a few questions, but probably not much, unless he's in the talking mood."

"How sad. I bet you've had to tell a lot of people that their loved one was murdered," I said, turning toward him.

"Oh yeah. Lots of times. It's not a part of the job I'm fond of. Fortunately, I'm no longer an officer, so that's out of my hands. I don't wish it on anyone though." He sighed, and a weary look crossed his face.

I agreed with him on that. I wouldn't wish it on anyone either.

Chapter Three

"JENNIFER, THERE'S SOMETHING I need to tell you," I said gently. She was sitting on the sofa, watching an old episode of *I Love Lucy*, with one eye on the television and one on her phone.

"What?" she asked without looking up.

I sat next to her and picked up the remote and turned the television off. She looked up from her phone, questioningly.

I sighed. "I have some bad news."

"What?" she asked, anxiety creeping into her voice.

"When Alec and I went into the woods, we stumbled upon a body," I said, trying to figure out how to make this easier. But the truth was, there wasn't going to be anything easy about this.

"Who was it?" she asked.

"Mrs. Rose," I said.

She gasped. "My teacher? Mom, I just saw her at Walmart a week and a half ago. There's no way!"

"I'm sorry, honey," I said.

She stared at me wide-eyed. "I just can't believe it. She asked me how college was. She said she was proud of me. She encouraged me and said I could do anything I wanted to do if I set my mind to it."

"She was a really good teacher," I said. "She was a good person."

She started crying, and I pulled her to me. All I could do was hold her.

IT WAS NICE BEING ABLE to ride over with Alec to interrogate a suspect without either begging him to take me along or having to hide the fact I was there so that his boss didn't jump all over him. Of course, the fact that I owned the car Alec was driving helped. It's not like he could tell me to stay home when he needed my car to get to the suspect.

"So, I've been thinking," I said, looking out the window as we drove along Allen Road. When Alec didn't answer, I continued. "I think now that you're no longer bound by the police department's rules and regulations, we should take a more aggressive stance on interrogating suspects. You know, really drill into them with the questions."

Alec chuckled. "I'm going to make you stay home."

"No, you can't. It's my car. Remember?"

"First off, you catch more flies with honey than with vinegar. Therefore, we will be nice and sweet to people. In the beginning, at least. Second of all, Mr. Rose is not a suspect. He is a grieving husband. We are not interrogating. We are merely interviewing and gathering information."

I snorted. "The husband always did it. It's a classic."

"Interviewing is a much sweeter word, don't you think?" he asked, ignoring my comment. "Besides, what if it was you that was being interviewed? Wouldn't you want someone to be nice? Especially if you didn't do it and you're grieving the loss of a loved one?"

"I know, you're right," I relented. "I just want to play good cop, bad cop one of these days. Will you let me do that?"

He chuckled again. "Yes. One day, when I'm relatively certain we are interviewing the bad guy, I'll let you play the bad cop."

"That's all I ask," I said.

I had no desire to be unkind to someone that was grieving the loss of a loved one. I knew about grieving all too well. My husband had been killed by a drunk driver, and my children's and my life had been changed forever. I did rather enjoy giving Alec a hard time about interrogating, though. I'd seen more than my share of old detective shows, and I liked the idea of being the bad cop. I doubted I could ever pull it off, though.

We pulled up to a modest-looking home in a family neighborhood on the Southside of town. Iris Rose lived in the Sandy Creek development, established in the early eighties. The homes were still kept up nicely and were smaller in size. It was the sort of area I would expect a schoolteacher to live.

Alec knocked on the door, and I could hear movement on the inside. I glanced at Alec. There were more sounds of movement from inside, but no one came to the door after several minutes. Alec rang the doorbell, and we heard more movement, then the door opened. A middle-aged man stood at the door, his hair uncombed, and dark circles under his bloodshot eyes. He looked like he had been through the mill. He seemed vaguely familiar, but I didn't think I had ever met Mr. Rose before.

"Mr. Rose?" Alec asked.

"Yeah," he said, nodding his head, looking from Alec to me.

"Mr. Rose, I'm De—Alec Blanchard," Alec said, stumbling over the fact that he was no longer a detective. I noticed a slight tenseness on his face when he said his name, and I wondered if losing his title bothered him more than he let on. He had been a detective for so many years, it had become his identity. "And this is Allie McSwain. We wanted to express our condolences on the loss of your wife, Iris. We're also working with the Sandy Harbor police department, and we'd like to have a word with you."

Mr. Rose looked from me to Alec again. "What do you mean? Working with the police department?"

"We were asked to interview you," Alec said, still not looking entirely comfortable with his new role as a non-detective. "We're investigating your wife's death."

"Alec is a retired detective with the police department, and now he's a private investigator," I supplied when Mr. Rose still looked at Alec blankly. "We're working with the police department."

It seemed like Mr. Rose was ready to tell us to hit the road, and I didn't want there to be any hostility between us before Alec got to interview him. It was only a small stretch of the truth that Alec was a private investigator. He would be one just as soon as he took the test to be licensed.

"Okay. Fine," Mr. Rose finally said, nodding his head. He stepped back, and we followed him into the living room. The house was decorated simply, and it felt warm and cozy in spite of the sparse décor.

"Have a seat," Mr. Rose said, motioning toward a sofa.

Alec and I sat, and he sat across from us on the love seat.

"Mr. Rose, I'm so sorry for your loss," I said quickly. "My daughter was in your wife's class the first year she was a teacher, and she loved Iris."

A wave of grief crossed his face, but he quickly recovered. "Thank you." He said thickly. "She loved the kids. She lived for them. I guess you never expect something like this. There's nothing that can prepare you for it."

"That's the truth," I said. "I know this is very hard."

"I'm sorry for your loss, Mr. Rose," Alec said. "Can you tell me, when was the last time you saw your wife?"

"It was two days ago. Sunday afternoon. She went to the school to work on grading papers."

"She was grading papers on a Sunday?" Alec asked, notebook and pen suddenly in hand.

"A teacher puts in a lot more than forty hours a week. She was there all the time," he explained. "The schools expect a lot. Lots of rules about everything."

"What time of day did she leave?" Alec asked.

"About noon. We went to church first, came home, and she was out the door again. She said she'd be home by four or five, but she never came back," he said, his voice cracking on the last part.

"What did you do then?" Alec asked.

"I called her cell phone, but there was no answer. Around six o'clock I started calling family members, friends. Anyone I could think of. No one had seen her. Around seven I drove by the school, but it was locked up. Then I called the police, but I was told she had to be missing for twenty-four hours before they would look into it. By the time the twenty-four hours were up, the police were coming to me," he said, staring at the floor.

I glanced at Alec. I didn't think he knew that we were the ones that had discovered her body. I wasn't sure if it would make a difference to him or not, but I thought we shouldn't mention it.

"Is there anyone you can think of that would want to hurt your wife?" Alec asked.

He shook his head. "No. No one. She was an elementary school teacher. She hung around people that were just like her. Other teachers."

"Mr. Rose, did you and your wife have any children?" I asked.

"No. Iris really didn't want any. Her childhood wasn't the greatest, and she didn't want to repeat it with kids of her own. Don't get me wrong, she loved kids, but she didn't want any of her own," he said, still looking down at his feet. "I was fine with it. I wanted what she wanted."

I wasn't sure I could identify with someone that didn't want children, but I figured it was better to know you didn't want them up front rather than figure it out after the fact.

"Did she have other family in town?" I asked. Other than Jennifer having had Iris as a teacher, I knew virtually nothing else about her.

He snorted. "Oh yeah. Her mother's a piece of work. I have never met another person that had such a need to control another person in my life."

Alec and I glanced at each other.

"How so?" Alec asked, scribbling in his notebook

"She tried to control everything. When Iris wanted to go to college, her mother wanted her to study to become a doctor. Iris always wanted to teach. Her mother wouldn't support her financially when she refused to go to med school. She wouldn't even help her fill out the financial aid papers. Then when Iris became a teacher, her mother was always trying to control that. Telling her how to decorate her classroom, telling her how to teach her students, telling her what to teach them. It never ended. There was this constant bickering between the two of them," he said. His face turned red as he spoke. The tension between the two of them was clear.

"And how about your marriage? Did your mother-in-law take a hands-off approach to that?" I asked, knowing that would be impossible if the woman were as controlling as he said she was.

He laughed, but there was no joy behind it. "She tried everything she could to keep us from getting married. She threatened to disown her. She told her she wouldn't come to the wedding. Then she tried to control us at every turn when Iris went with her heart and married me anyway. She was always telling her how to behave in our marriage. She was obsessed with having grandchildren, so she was always looking up all these natural remedies for infertility. She made Iris a tea that she said was for her eczema, but it made Iris sick for three days. Later she admitted it was a fertility tea and refused to tell her what was in it. Iris refused to drink any more of it, and Hilda went into a rage, demanding she drink it so she would get pregnant," he said. "The crazy part was she wasn't infertile, she just didn't want kids. But Hilda wouldn't listen."

"Hilda is her mother? Did she have these rages often?" I asked.

He nodded. "Oh yeah. Whenever she didn't get her way."

"What's her last name, and how can we get ahold of her?" Alec asked.

"Her last name's Bixby, and she lives in the apartment over my garage."

Chapter Four

"WAIT—YOUR MOTHER-IN-law, who is controlling and seems to have made you and your wife very unhappy, is living in an apartment above your garage?" I asked. It didn't make sense. I had gotten along fine with my mother-in-law, but there was no way I would have wanted her living that close to me.

"Yeah, I know," he said. "It doesn't make sense. I told my wife it was a bad idea, and believe me, it was. But Iris insisted. Hilda could guilt her into anything. She would just pop in here whenever she wanted. No knocking. Just pop in and stick her nose into whatever my wife and I were doing."

My mind spun with the thought. I could imagine how normal marital disagreements could be turned into family brawls with a family that was already on the edge. And if what Richard Rose was saying was true, this was a family on the edge.

"You know what I think?" he asked. "I think Hilda was jealous of Iris. She had a really bad childhood, and when her husband dumped her, I think it was the epitome of failure to her. She would have loved for her daughter's marriage to have failed, too."

The muscle along Mr. Rose's jawline twitched. I looked at Alec, unsure of what to say next.

"Do you think Iris's mother killed her?" Alec asked flatly.

He nodded his head. "I do. She went down to the school on Sunday when I told her Iris was there working. She had to stick her nose into whatever Iris was working on. Hilda came back, but Iris didn't."

"I think we should go and have a talk with her," Alec said. "Thank you for your time, Mr. Rose. We'll be in touch."

Mr. Rose led us to the front door, and we said our goodbyes.

"Wow," I said when he had closed the door. "I know they must have had their problems, but I can't imagine a mother killing her child."

Alec looked at me. "Do you ever watch the news? Parents kill their own children all the time."

I breathed out hard. "I know, I know. But I can't imagine it. I just can't."

We walked around the side of the house and to the detached garage. There was a dark blue Toyota parked beneath a landing that led to the apartment. I wondered how old Iris's mother was because the steps were steep and narrow. I figured at least mid to late sixties based on how old I thought Iris was, but maybe she was in good shape physically and didn't have an issue with the stairs.

"Up we go," Alec said, and we began climbing. I was glad I was a runner. These things would wear you out if you had to climb them every day.

Alec barely had time to rap out two knocks before the door swung open. Hilda Bixby stood at the door, her gray hair in a bun on the top of her hair, and her eyes red and swollen.

"Good morning, Mrs. Bixby," Alec said, "I'm Alec Blanchard, and this is Allie McSwain. We're working with the Sandy Harbor police department and we'd like to have a few minutes of your time."

She looked from Alec to me and back to Alec without saying a word.

"Mrs. Bixby, we just wanted to express how sorry we were to hear about your daughter, Iris. She was my daughter's second grade teacher, the first year she taught," I said, giving her a sympathetic look. I could use some sugar when I needed to.

Mrs. Bixby took a deep breath. "Come in," she said and led us into the apartment. The apartment was small, but Mrs. Bixby had made good use of the space, with slightly undersized furnishings. There were floral prints everywhere, but she had somehow managed to keep them from feeling overwhelming. Mrs. Bixby had a flair for decorating.

"Please, sit. Would you like some tea or coffee?" she asked stiffly.

"No, thank you," Alec said before I could answer. We sat down on a loveseat across from her. "Mrs. Bixby, we'd like to ask you a few questions. Do you know of anyone that would want to harm your daughter?"

"I certainly do," Mrs. Bixby said confidently.

"And who would that be?" Alec asked.

"My son-in-law, Richard Rose," she said with a gleam in her eye.

"And why would you suspect him?" Alec asked, notebook, and pen in hand.

"Because he wanted to get rid of her. She had infertility problems. It broke Iris's heart. She wanted children so badly. It was easier for him to get rid of her and find a new wife that could have children than to go through a divorce."

I forced myself not to look in Alec's direction. This was the opposite of what Richard Rose had told us.

Alec scribbled in his notebook, then looked up at her. "Not being able to have children isn't usually a reason to kill someone. Was there anything else going on?"

She nodded smugly. "Richard also had an affair."

Mr. Rose had forgotten to tell us this little tidbit of information.

"Are you certain?" Alec asked, scribbling in his book.

"Of course I am. Iris found out about it. Richard's a high school teacher and he had an affair with a student. Janice Cross. Later she went off to college and became a second grade teacher. Just Like Iris. It wouldn't surprise me one bit if he ends up marrying her."

Alec looked up at her. "Was Janice still in high school when the affair occurred?"

"He said it didn't begin until the summer after she graduated, but why would anyone believe him?" she said bitterly. "He's a born liar, that one is."

"Did Janice Cross work at the same school that Iris did?" I asked, hoping she didn't.

"Oh yes. You know it tormented her every time she had to see that woman at work. I told her not to marry Richard. That he would only bring her misery. First, he tormented her for not being able to get pregnant and have the children she wanted so desperately. And then he had an affair," she said and broke down crying. "My poor baby."

I reached for the box of tissues on the end table and handed them to her. "I'm so sorry, Hilda. I know this is hard."

She looked at me sharply. "You know, as a mother, it's a nightmare. My daughter didn't deserve this. That monster is living free, right over there, and that's not right. He's the one that deserved to die out in those woods, not her." Her face tightened up in anger.

Richard Rose was right about one thing. She had a temper.

"A lot of people have affairs, and while it's not right, they don't usually want to murder their spouses," Alec said gently. "Why, specifically, do you think he would murder her as opposed to divorcing her?"

Janice sighed loudly. "Because it's easier. Why go to court, when you can just end the marriage this way? There's just no accounting for why people do the things they do."

Hilda wasn't making sense. I glanced at Alec and could see his brow furrow.

"Is there anything else we need to know?" he asked.

"Just that Richard is an evil man. You have to keep your eye on him. Iris didn't have an enemy in this world. If you had known my daughter, you would know that everyone that knew her, loved her," she said, now completely dry-eyed. She turned toward me. "Isn't it true that your daughter loved her when she was in her class?"

I nodded. There was no denying it. Iris Rose had had a way with kids. "Absolutely. She talked about her all the time."

She looked at Alec and nodded triumphantly.

"Mrs. Bixby, where were you on Sunday?" Alec asked without skipping a beat.

Janice's eyes got big. "I went to the school to help my daughter. She had papers to grade, and I always helped her out. I don't know how she would have managed to do her job if it wasn't for me helping her. That school demands so much of its teachers. And she really appreciated it. She said so all the time."

"What time did you leave?" Alec asked.

"Oh, I don't know. Around 2:30, if I remember right."

"And did Iris stay late?" he asked, making notes.

"Yes. Iris said she had a few more things to do, and she would be home in an hour or so. But she never showed up," she said, and her voice cracked.

My heart went out to Hilda. She may have been a difficult person, but she was grieving for her daughter.

"Thank you, Mrs. Bixby. If you think of anything else, please give me a call," he said and handed her his card. "And we'll be in touch."

We left Hilda and climbed down the stairs, hanging onto the handrail so we didn't take a tumble. I would not have liked having to navigate those stairs every day, especially with as much snow as we got each year.

"So what do you think?" I asked when we got back into the car.

He sighed and shook his head. "I don't know at this point. Mrs. Bixby is a little off if you ask me."

"She might be an oddball, but that doesn't mean she's a murderer. I think she's just grieving the loss of her daughter. And why didn't Richard mention his affair?" I asked.

"I don't know. Maybe he didn't think it was relevant."

"I think things like that become relevant when there's a murder involved," I pointed out.

"True, but if he really dated Janice Cross around the time she was in high school, and now she's been through college and is a teacher, it's been a while ago, and he may not have thought it was important," he said, pulling away from the curb. "One thing's for sure. They both have very different views of what Iris felt for her mother."

"That's for sure. Richard sees Hilda as being controlling, and Hilda sees her actions as being helpful," I said.

"We'll have to see how this all plays out. It's too early to point the finger at anyone."

That was true, but I had a finger that I wanted to point, and I really couldn't make up my mind about either one of them.

Chapter Five

"SO, HOW'S IT GOING?" I asked Alec. He was sitting at my kitchen table with his nose in a book, studying for his PI license. His eyebrows were furrowed and his lips moved as he read. I figured it would be easy as pie for him to pass, but he was a worrywart and insisted on studying.

"Just fine, thanks," he said, not looking up from his book.

I opened a cupboard door and stared into it, trying to decide on something to bake. I had ended my blog on grief, and I needed something to do with my life. I had considered a food blog, and it was still a possibility, but if I was going to write about baking, I needed to bake.

"How does blueberry sour cream pie sound?" I asked.

"Sounds good," he mumbled.

I looked over my shoulder at him. "A little more enthusiasm?"

He looked up at me. "Yum. Blueberries." Then he went back to his book.

"Gee, thanks," I said. The doorbell rang. "I'll get it."

"Hey, Lucy," I said when I opened the door.

"Hey, Allie, what's up? I heard Iris Rose was murdered! I know you have to know something. Spill it! I need the scoop," she said.

I put my finger to my lips and stepped back, letting her in. "Alec's in the kitchen."

She closed the door behind herself, and we headed for my bedroom. I knew Alec knew I was going to tell Lucy everything, but I still didn't want him to hear me tell it.

"We found her buried in the snow out in the woods. We've talked to her husband and mother, and they both blame each other. Other than that, nothing else has happened," I whispered.

"What? You found her? When? Why didn't you tell me sooner?" she exclaimed, taking her white knit hat off. Her blond hair was a little wild this morning, and I reached out and pushed a lock of it down. "Stop it," she said, slapping my hand.

"Monday. We were going out to collect snow for snow cream, and I unburied her," I said, looking away. The thought of eating the snow that was covering her still sickened me.

"Monday? And you didn't call me? What's up with that?" she asked, sitting on the edge of my bed.

I sighed. "I don't know. It all happened so fast. And it was kind of gross, you know?" I said.

"Oh. Was she, like, messed up?" she asked.

I shook my head. "No, I was scooping up the snow that covered her for our snow cream."

"Oh," she said, making a face. "So how did she die?"

"We don't know yet. There wasn't anything apparent when we found her. Did you know her?"

She shook her head. "No, but her husband worked part-time at the newspaper with Ed about fifteen years ago. We went out for drinks once, but Iris had to work if I remember right. He seemed like a nice guy."

"I thought he was a teacher at the high school?"

"He is. I guess they needed the money because he only worked a couple of hours a day in the late afternoons," she said.

"How about her mother, Hilda Bixby? Do you know her?"

Her eyebrows furrowed. "Didn't she work at the Bank of Maine years ago?"

I shrugged. "I'm not sure. We didn't ask."

"I think she did, and as I recall, I always thought she was a little off. Just kind of weird, you know? It seemed like there was someplace else she worked, too, but I can't remember where," she said.

"Weird how?" I asked.

"She would ask personal questions when she waited on me. Personal for a teller-customer relationship, you know? Like who my husband was, did I love him, and did we have kids and—I don't know. It always seemed like she *really* wanted to know the answer. I don't know her well though, so who knows?"

"Well, that's all I know about it," I said. "And now, I'm going to figure out something to bake. Want to help?"

"I thought you'd never ask. I am still trying to forgive you for going to Alabama for Christmas. I missed out on all those holiday treats," she said, following me into the kitchen.

"You'll live," I said over my shoulder.

"Hi, Alec," she said. "What are you doing?"

"Studying for my PI license," he said, looking up from his book.

"I don't understand why you need to study," I said, opening the refrigerator door.

"Because the state of Maine has laws and regulations that apply differently for a PI than for a police officer, and I'd like to not cross them," he said, getting up and pouring himself a cup of coffee. "Lucy, there's coffee if you'd like some."

Lucy got a cup out of the cupboard and poured herself a cup of coffee.

"I think I know what I'm going to do," I said.

"Yes?" Lucy asked.

"Yes. I think I'm going to write a baking blog, and also, since I need to be baking all the time, I think I'm going to see if any of the local restaurants around here would be interested in selling some of my desserts. Otherwise, I'm going to eat far more of them than I need to," I said. The idea had just occurred to me, and it seemed like a good one.

"Oh wow, who would have thought of you selling your pies at a local restaurant? What a novel idea!" Lucy said. Her words dripped with sarcasm.

I gave her the evil eye. In September she had made the same suggestion to me, minus the blog. Reluctantly, I had baked up the perfect apple pie and taken it to Henry Hoffer to try, with the hopes that he would sell my pies in his restaurant, Henry's Home Cooking Restaurant. Unfortunately, when I went to check on how he liked the pie the next day, I found Henry dead. Someone had plunged a knife into his chest. Let's just say I was a little soured on the idea of baking for his restaurant after that.

But that was several months ago, and his widow had taken over the restaurant. I was ready to try again. I had checked on her once after Henry's murder and hadn't been back since. The rumor around town was that she had redecorated, changed the menu, and really turned the restaurant around and was now doing a brisk business. It might be a good relationship if I could get my pies and maybe some cakes onto the menu.

"So how does a blueberry sour cream pie sound?" I asked her.

"It sounds like I need to stick around to see how this turns out," she said with a grin.

I took out some sour cream, blueberries, and eggs from the refrigerator and then moved to the cupboards.

Lucy sat at the table across from Alec while I assembled everything.

"So Alec, how do you like retirement?" she asked.

"Well, I didn't get much time off in the way of retirement, seeing as how we discovered a body less than a week after I retired. But other than that, I'm doing just fine," he said.

"At least there's none of that police paperwork, right?" she asked. "And no annoying co-workers."

He sat back in his chair and nodded. "There is that. Not having paperwork frees up a lot of my time. Plus, I can set my own schedule. What's not to love about that?"

I looked over my shoulder and saw her lean closer to Alec and whisper. "So Alec, when do you move in?"

He smiled and glanced at me. "The way things are going, I'd say never."

"What?" she said loudly and looked at me. "What's wrong? I thought you two were all cutesy-cutesy kissy-kissy together. What's going on?"

"Nothing is going on," I said. "You know how I am."

"What? How are you?" she asked.

"She's old fashioned," Alec supplied. "And I like old fashioned."

"Aw," Lucy said. "That's so sweet. See, you guys *are* cutesy."

"We are not cutesy, Lucy Gray. And this isn't any of your business," I warned.

She gasped. "Okay, okay. I won't pry. Much. But I expect to be informed of all the details as they occur."

I rolled my eyes. "See what I got you into, Alec?"

"I do see it. Now I'm going to go into the other room so I can study," he said, standing up and picking up his book.

"Ah, are you saying I'm loud?" Lucy asked as he left the room.

"Yup," he called over his shoulder.

She looked at me. "He's so cute."

"I know," I agreed. Alec was the best thing that had happened to me in a long time.

Chapter Six

"I DON'T KNOW WHAT SHE looks like. How are we going to know it's her?" I asked Alec as we pulled up to Belmont elementary school.

"We'll figure something out," he said, shutting off the engine. He looked at me with those dark blue eyes and smiled at me. "It's called detective work."

I smiled back at him and wondered what our children might have looked like if we had met earlier. Him with his black hair and dark blue eyes and me with my red hair and green eyes. I pushed the thought away guiltily. I would never have wanted to miss out on being with my husband, Thaddeus, or the two beautiful children we had had. Life was as it was supposed to be.

The hallways of the school were nearly empty. We passed a mother with her daughter in tow and a couple of adults that must have been teachers or admin staff.

"See?" Alec said, pointing at classroom door number five. Beneath the number was the teacher's name, Mrs. Johnson.

"I see," I said, and we kept walking.

We passed another man and six more doors and came to classroom number twelve and the name, Ms. Cross.

Alec opened the door without knocking and a young woman at the big desk at the front of the classroom looked up.

"May I help you?" she asked. She had a stack of papers on her desk in front of her and she looked surprised to see us.

Ms. Cross was blond and fair-skinned and pretty. Model pretty. It was easy to see why Richard Rose had fallen for her.

"Yes, we're working with the police department," Alec said and introduced us. "Can we have a few minutes of your time?"

Janice's face went pale. Paler than it already was.

"Of course," she said and forced herself to smile. "Sorry, I only have small people chairs."

"Oh, that's okay," I said and grabbed two chairs from the closest desks, and set them in front of her desk. Alec and I sat down and looked up at her. "Wow, talk about a different perspective."

She smiled at me and then turned to Alec. "What can I help you with?"

"I'm assuming you've heard about Iris Rose?" he asked.

"Oh, yes. It's so tragic. Really, she was such a nice person and a wonderful teacher. Her students are heartsick."

"They know already?" I asked. I don't know what I expected, but it surprised me.

"Yes, the principal broke it to them today. No details, of course. It would frighten them to know their teacher had been, well, murdered," she said with a frown.

"I'm sure it would. Are there counselors for them? In case they need to talk to someone?" I asked.

"Definitely. We have two on loan from another district," she said, glancing at Alec.

"Ms. Cross, do you know of anyone that might want to hurt Iris?" Alec asked. He already had his notebook and pen out.

She shook her head, wide-eyed. "I have no idea. Like I said, she was well-liked."

"Did you know Iris's husband, Richard?" he asked. Just like that. I expected him to beat around the bush, but he just threw it out there.

Her face went white. She opened her mouth to speak, and stumbled over the words, then she closed her mouth and looked down at her hands. After a moment, she cleared her throat. "I do," she said, looking up at me. "Richard and I had an affair. I suppose you already know that. It didn't last long, and it was a few years ago." She looked up at him, her eyes wet from unshed tears, and I couldn't tell if it was because the affair had been short-lived or she was embarrassed it had occurred in the first place.

"Who broke up with whom?" Alec asked, showing no emotion.

"I broke up with him. I never felt right about it and I couldn't stand the lie," she said. "Plus, I went away to college." She looked down when she said that part.

"How old were you when the affair started?" Alec asked.

"Oh, I was eighteen. I had just turned eighteen when we started seeing each other. It didn't last long. Three months, and then I was off to college," she said quickly.

I couldn't help but wonder if the affair would have continued if she hadn't left town.

"How did Iris find out about it?" I asked.

She looked at a spot on the desk in front of her, quiet for a moment. "I guess she might have suspected he was running around on her," she said, looking up at me. "Then when I got a job here, she came to help the new teacher decorate her class. And I had brought a box of items from home, a corkboard, art supplies, and pictures. And there was a picture of Richard and me in the box."

I gasped, horrified at the thought. "And she found it. Wow," I said.

She looked up at me, and now the tears spilled down her cheeks, and she grabbed for a tissue from the box on her desk. "She was a good person. She came to help out the new teacher, you know? She was the only one that did. I swear I thought I had gotten rid of all those pictures. I swear. The relationship had ended years earlier."

I nodded slowly. I could never imagine dating a married man, but to have his wife discover the truth in such an "in your face" way? How devastating. I breathed in deeply.

"What did she do?" I asked.

She shook her head slowly. "She just looked at me with so much hurt in her eyes. She backed out of the room without saying a word."

Alec was making notes again, and for once, I wished he'd stop. I wanted to hate this woman for what she had done, but she didn't seem like a terrible person. Young and stupid, yes. But not a murderer.

Finally, Alec looked up at her. "Is there anything else you want to tell us?"

"No, not really," she said, looking away.

"When was the last time you saw Iris?" he asked.

"At school on Friday," she said. "Can you believe she brought me some construction paper? She'd found it on sale at a really good price and bought extra. She gave me some of it."

"She does sound like she was a nice person," I said.

"There are regrets you have in life. Things that you wish you could take back," she said.

"That's for sure," Alec said, nodding.

"Oh, you know what?" she suddenly said. "I just remembered. There was construction paper scattered on the floor in the hallway when I came in on Monday. The same construction paper Iris bought."

"A lot?" I asked.

"Maybe around twenty-five to thirty sheets? And some crayons. I thought maybe one of the kids had made a mess and got scared and left it there without telling anyone. Some kids are really shy, and they're afraid to tell anyone if they think they'll get in trouble."

Alec looked at her, thinking. "Where in the hallway?"

"I'll show you," she said, standing up and leading the way.

We followed her out into the hallway.

"There," she said, going to the stairwell and pointing down. "At the bottom of the stairs."

A rope hung across the stairs, with a sign that said *no admittance*.

"What's down there?" I asked.

"Classrooms that we don't use. I guess at one, time the school had so many kids enrolled that they built classrooms in the basement. The teacher's lounge is also down there, and that's why I figured one of the kids was down there when they knew they shouldn't have been. Some kids panic when they do something they know is wrong, and I figured they just left the paper and crayons."

"You don't mind if we have a look?" Alec asked.

"No, help yourself," she said, and Alec unhooked the rope, and we started down the stairs. Janice flipped on a light so we could see and followed us down. There wasn't anything unusual at the bottom of the steps.

"The paper and crayons were laying here," she said, pointing to the floor.

Alec looked around the area, then took his phone out and took pictures. I couldn't see anything worth taking pictures of, but he was the professional. Across the hall was the teacher's lounge, and I walked over and pushed the door open.

The lounge had an assortment of tables, chairs, and a sofa and overstuffed chairs. One wall had a row of cupboards with a microwave on the counter and a refrigerator in the corner. There was nothing exciting in here, but I remembered thinking the teacher's lounge was some mysterious hall of adulthood that I was afraid to enter when I was in elementary school. I could see a kid sneaking down here and getting scared of being caught, then leaving everything behind if they heard someone approaching.

Alec joined me in the lounge.

"Nothing exciting," I said with a shrug.

He walked around, looking at everything, and opening cupboard doors. "I think you might be right about that."

We left the lounge, and Janice was waiting just outside the door. "Okay?" she asked.

Alec nodded. "Thanks for all your help," he said. "If you think of anything, will you give me a call?" he asked and handed her a business card.

"Yes, I will," she said and headed back down the hall.

"Those are your police detective business cards, aren't they?" I asked as we walked down the hall.

He smiled. "I have a lot of them. Besides, I never said I was a detective, I just said I was working for the police department."

Chapter Seven

JANICE WENT BACK INTO her classroom, and as soon as she was out of sight, Alec pulled me down another hallway.

"What are you doing?" I whispered.

"Iris Rose's classroom has to be here somewhere," he said, looking at the names on the door.

We kept walking and finally found it at the end of the hall. "Voila," I said. "You're so smart."

"I prefer to call it experienced," he said.

"And it looks like someone's home," I whispered. The door stood ajar, and the light was on.

Alec pulled the door open, and we were surprised to see Richard Rose sitting at Iris's desk. His eyes opened wide when he saw us.

"Hello Mr. Rose," Alec said.

He gave us a sad, lopsided smile. "Hello, Detective, Mrs. McSwain."

"Allie," I offered. We approached the big desk. "How are you doing?"

He sighed tiredly. His eyes were red and swollen, and I couldn't help but feel he couldn't have committed the murder. He seemed like he was genuinely grieving his wife's death.

"I came to clean out Iris's classroom. Mrs. Decker, the principal, offered to do it for me, but I wanted to do it," he said. There were three empty paper boxes next to the desk and from the looks of it he hadn't gotten started yet.

"I'm sure that's a very difficult job," I said.

He nodded slowly. "Harder than I had imagined."

"Would you like some help?" Alec asked.

I looked in his direction. I knew he wanted a look around the place in hopes there would be something that would give him some clues to her murder.

Richard opened his mouth to say something and then closed it. After a moment, he said, "I suppose it might be helpful."

I walked over and picked up two of the empty paper boxes and handed one to Alec. The classroom was done in winter scenes with four corkboards displaying posters featuring cartoon characters reminding students to use their manners, don't do drugs, and grammatical parts of a sentence. I smiled. The best part of elementary school had been when the teacher decorated the classroom for holidays and the changing seasons. Christmas was over, and Valentine's Day was still over a month away, so Iris had chosen winter scenes. I loved the green and blue plaid mittens and red sled cutouts. I thought Iris probably had a pretty happy classroom. The children would miss her.

"Do you want me to take down the cutouts?" I asked, looking over my shoulder at Richard, who was still sitting behind Iris's desk.

"No, those can stay. There are some personal pictures on that one board. We went out into the woods and took pictures of as much wildlife as we could find, and she brought them here for the kids. That day holds a lot of memories for me. I'd like to have them," he said sadly.

"You got it," I said and went over to the board and began unpinning the pictures.

"Are these pictures of other teachers?" Alec asked from his side of the classroom.

"Yeah, that was during a Christmas party one year. You can leave those. They hold memories for people here."

I wondered if Janice was in those pictures, but I couldn't ask in front of Richard. Alec would tell me later. I wondered how Iris felt about having to work with her husband's lover. I know how I would feel. And it wasn't warm and fuzzy.

Richard pulled open the top drawer of her desk and pulled out a plastic world globe and began sobbing quietly. I looked at Alec, who gave me a terrified look. Men were terrible at handling other men's emotions. I went to him and squeezed his shoulder.

"You don't have to do this, Richard. Let Alec and I pack things up. You go on home and we'll bring them by your house," I said.

He shook his head. "You don't know what to pack," he sobbed.

"If we pack things you don't want, we'll bring them back here for you. I promise we won't leave anything behind that looks even the least bit important."

He shook his head. "I just can't believe it. Who would do something like this?" he looked up into my eyes and at the moment I wished more than anything that I could give him an answer.

"I don't know. I'm so sorry," I said. I felt my chest tighten and tears sprang to my eyes. I blinked them back. Richard didn't need me breaking down in front of him, and Alec might freak if he had to deal with both of us crying.

"It doesn't make any sense," he said. "Everyone liked Iris."

"No, it doesn't. I really wish you'd let us handle this for you. It might be easier for you to look through these things by yourself," I said gently.

I grabbed a couple of tissues from the box on Iris's desk and handed them to him.

"Maybe you're right," he said, taking the tissues from me. He slowly stood up from the chair. "I'm sorry to do this to you."

"It's no problem," I said. I desperately wanted to hug him, but it seemed inappropriate. I didn't know him.

But maybe I could be the official hugger that went along with Alec on investigations. I glanced at Alec, who had his nose to a bulletin board. I doubted he would care for that. I turned back to Richard. "You get home and get some rest, and we'll bring you Iris's things."

He nodded. "Okay, thank you. I can't thank you two enough, really."

"No thanks needed," I said and walked him to the door. He left without looking back, and I closed the door behind him.

"That is so sad," I said.

Alec nodded, having taken the seat that Richard had vacated. I picked up one of the student seats and sat it next to him as he pulled open a drawer. Alec sorted through it, but it only held school supplies.

"So, with Janice right down the hall, what are the chances he's going to stop off and say hello?" Alec asked in a lowered tone.

I gasped. "Do you think?"

"Well, he's free now," he said.

"That's so rude," I said in disbelief.

He shrugged. "Maybe so. And he could be perfectly innocent, but it is convenient."

"Should I go peek and see if he stopped by her classroom?" I asked.

"No, it would be bad if you got caught."

"Between Richard, Janice, and Iris's mother, who do you think is most likely?" I asked him while searching through a small side drawer.

He grinned. "I think it's far too early to know. We don't even know how she died yet. But if I had to make a guess, I'm going with her mother."

"What? Why? That doesn't make sense," I said.

"Are you still hung up on thinking a mother wouldn't murder her own child? That's been proven to be wrong over and over," he said, pulling out a book.

"What's that?" I asked. "And yes, I'm going with my theory that a mother wouldn't kill her children, at least not in most cases. Those times when it has happened, well, those are just freak women that never should have had children."

"I agree on that point," he said, flipping pages in the book. "This appears to be a journal."

"Really? Why would she keep it here?" I asked. "Maybe she didn't want Richard to find it?"

There had to be something juicy in it, otherwise, why would it be here at school?

"I doubt it. It looks like she kept a journal of her day. She's talking about the kids and what she taught and also some problem behaviors in a couple of the kids," he said and turned the page.

I sighed. "I guess that makes sense. This desk doesn't lock, and it would be right there for anyone to read."

He looked up at me. "And what is your theory?"

"I honestly don't know. I don't want to think either Richard or Janice are involved. They don't seem the type," I said, pulling out a bead bracelet. "This is cute." It had beads and crystals on it, but it was obviously not expensive.

"It is," he said absently.

"Did you ever run across a murderer that seemed completely innocent, but then you found out they were guilty?" I asked him. "I mean, no negative feelings about them at all? Not even a hint?"

He chuckled. "That happens more often than you'd think. Although most people do give themselves away eventually. But it happens. And there's one thing you don't seem to have thought about."

"What?" I asked. I had no idea what he was talking about. I thought I was becoming a very good detective.

"Those tears from Richard could be tears of remorse. Maybe he's grieving the fact that he couldn't control himself in the heat of an argument. Maybe he did kill her and feels guilty."

I gasped. He was right, I hadn't thought of that. "Do you think that's it?"

He shrugged. "I have no idea. We have a lot more investigating to do."

"I want you to admit something," I said.

He looked at me. "What?"

"That you love having me along for investigations."

He tipped his head back and laughed a lot harder than he should have.

"What is so funny?" I asked, narrowing my eyes at him.

"You. You're so funny," he said, returning to reading the journal.

"Excuse me, mister. I am not funny. I'm being serious."

"Yeah, I know. That's what makes it even funnier," he said with a smirk.

I breathed out hard. Some people.

Chapter Eight

IT TOOK US JUST OVER an hour to pack up everything that looked like it might have some sentimental value to Richard, including the journal. I had taken the liberty of reading a few entries and was touched by her care for her students. I thought it would make Richard happy to be able to read through it and remember how sweet Iris had been. Sadly, we hadn't found anything that would be of use to us in the investigation into Iris's death. I had hoped there would be something.

We put the lids on the boxes, and Alec put the fern she had had on her desk on top of one of the boxes and picked it up. The door swung open, and a young man with dark-rimmed glasses stopped in his tracks and stared at us. He held a bouquet of red roses in his hand, and his black hair was slicked down.

"Oh, I'm sorry. I didn't, uh, mean to disturb anyone," he said looking at the floor.

"Oh, no problem," I said and smiled at him. "We were just packing up Mrs. Rose's belongings to take to her husband, Richard."

Alec gave me a look and set the box and fern down on the desk. He strode over to the young man with his hand extended. "Alec Blanchard," he said.

The young man gave him a deer-in-the-headlights look. He stood in front of Alec, not offering him his hand. Alec smiled bigger.

"And you are?" Alec asked, still extending his hand.

The young man rubbed his right hand on his coat and then stuck it out to shake Alec's hand. "Uh, Josh. Josh, uh, Stine." He looked away from Alec. He had a slight build, and his face was broken out in severe acne. I thought he must be around eighteen or nineteen at the most.

"Did you know Mrs. Rose?" Alec asked him amiably.

Josh looked up at him. Alec was at least six inches taller than he was. His face turned red, and he stammered. "Yes. I uh, she was, well, she was my—my teacher. Once. A long time ago," he said, nodding his head, but not meeting Alec's gaze.

"Really? So did Allie's daughter, Jennifer," Alec said, including me in the conversation.

I crossed the room and held my hand out to him. "I'm Allie McSwain. When was Mrs. Rose your teacher?"

"Oh, um, a long time ago," he repeated and wiped his hand on his coat again and then shook my hand. His hand was slightly damp, and his grip was weak.

"Did you know my daughter? You look like you might be about her age. Jennifer McSwain?" I asked him.

He looked at me and focused his eyes on me. "Yeah, I did. I mean, we weren't friends or anything. But I went to school with her."

I smiled at him, hoping to make him more comfortable. He seemed very nervous. His left hand squeezed the bouquet of roses.

"I thought you looked like you were about her age," I said brightly. "I almost think I remember you from some school function. Did you sing in the choir?"

"What?" he asked, wide-eyed. "N-no—I don't sing. I can't sing."

"Oh, okay, my mistake," I said. "Did you bring the flowers for Mrs. Rose?"

He remembered the flowers when I mentioned them, and he looked down, his jaw twitching. Did he know she was dead? He had to, didn't he?

He finally nodded slowly. "Yes. I brought them for her." He looked up at me. "I mean, I know she's—she's gone. But I brought them for her."

I nodded sympathetically. "I'm so sorry. Jennifer was shocked, too. Mrs. Rose meant a lot to Jennifer. She must have meant a lot to you, too."

His eyes filled with unshed tears. "She was the best teacher in the whole world. And she was pretty. She always encouraged me. And really, really nice. She was always nice to me."

"It's such a shame. I can't think of another person less deserving of dying so young," I said and glanced at Alec.

"Josh, when was the last time you talked to Mrs. Rose?" Alec asked lightly.

Josh turned toward him. "I guess a couple of weeks ago," he said with a shrug.

"Oh, so you kept in contact with her after you left school?" he asked.

"Not exactly. But I moved back to town recently. I had gone to college in Houston, but uh, my mother, she got sick and needed my help," he said evenly. "I stopped in to say hello to Mrs. Rose a couple of weeks ago. It was good to see her."

"So you moved back to Sandy Harbor to help your mom?" I asked.

He nodded. "Only for a while. Until she gets to feeling better. I'm going to study and take classes online until next fall."

He said the last part with a note of pride in his voice. He was a curious person, and I racked my mind, trying to remember if Jennifer had ever mentioned him to me. I could have sworn I had seen him at some school function, but I was drawing a blank.

"Do you think someone is going to take over her class?" he asked.

"Oh, I would imagine. Or maybe they'll split the kids up among the current teachers. I would imagine it takes a while to hire a new teacher," I said.

"Split them up?" he said and pushed his glasses up on his nose. "That isn't a good idea. Those kids need each other. Especially after losing Mrs. Rose."

"Well, maybe they'll hire a substitute, and that way they can all stay together, right here in this classroom," I suggested. I glanced at Alec, who was watching Josh intently.

"That's a good idea," Josh said, and he started walking slowly toward Iris's desk. "She was the best teacher in the whole world."

"We've heard the same thing from other people," Alec said.

"Would you like a vase to put those flowers in?" I asked and moved over to the corner of the classroom. There was a cupboard and a sink there, and I had seen a vase beneath the sink when we were packing. I pulled it out and showed it to him.

He almost smiled. "That would be nice."

"Here, let me have them, and I'll take care of them for you," I said, stepping toward him.

He looked at the flowers again and then handed them to me. I took them to the sink and carefully unwrapped them and arranged them in the vase.

"Josh, have you lived in Sandy Harbor all your life?" Alec asked pleasantly.

"Yes, I have. All my life. Except for when I moved to Houston for a little while."

"Do I know your mom and dad?" I asked, turning the faucet on for the flowers.

"I doubt it. My mother doesn't work, and I have never met my father," he said darkly.

"Oh, I see," I said. I would have to ask Jennifer about him and his mother. He seemed nice enough, even if he was a little odd. "There, how does that look?" I asked, holding the vase up for his inspection.

Josh beamed. "That looks really nice. You have a real talent there with flowers, Mrs. McSwain."

I laughed. "I wouldn't call it a talent, and you can call me Allie."

He nodded. "I like this classroom. I remember it really well. I just wish she didn't die."

"I'm sure she was thrilled to see you again," I said sympathetically. "You're a good person for remembering her and wanting to catch up with her. I'm sure teachers love it when that happens."

"You think so?" he asked.

"I do," I said and set the vase of flowers on Iris's desk.

He looked at me, smiling. "Well, I better get going. My mom's expecting me home soon. Thanks for helping with the flowers."

"You're welcome. And I'm sorry for your loss, Josh," I said.

"Thanks," he said and walked slowly toward the door. He looked over his shoulder before pushing the door open. "Thanks again."

When the door swung closed, Alec looked at me. "You think Iris really was thrilled when kids turned back up?"

"Of course I do! Don't you think it's satisfying to see the kids you nurtured years ago, grow up, and go to college? Look at him. He's responsible enough to help his mom out and still keep up with his studies. That's a fine young man right there."

"But you're going to ask Jennifer about him, aren't you?" he asked, picking up the box he had previously set down.

"Oh, you bet ya. I just know I've seen that kid somewhere, but I can't remember where."

He chuckled. "Come on, super sleuth. We gotta get a move on. Richard is waiting for this stuff."

"That's Ms. Super Sleuth to you, sir."

Chapter Nine

I LOOKED AT LUCY, SITTING next to me.

"What if she doesn't like them?" I asked.

"What?" she asked, buckling her seat belt. "She'd be crazy not to. Who wouldn't like whatever you baked? I mean, seriously. It doesn't matter what it is, it's delectable."

"That's a big word for you," I said, starting the car and giving her a big grin.

"Watch it, Red," she said and elbowed me in the side.

I giggled. "What if it's too much for me to do? I mean, I love baking, but what if it's so much work that I can't handle it? I can't spend all my time in the kitchen. I have a life to live, too. Where will I find the time to spend with Alec?"

"Then don't over-promise. Negotiate. When you feel confident, you can do what you've offered, and when you feel you can do more, then do more. But not until then."

"Right. You're exactly right," I said and pulled away.

"What's the latest on Iris Rose?" she asked, flipping the visor down in front of her and checking her makeup.

"Well, let me update you on the way over," I said.

We were headed to Henry's Home Cooking Restaurant to speak to Cynthia Hoffer. I had heard nothing but good things about the changes Cynthia had made down there since taking over after the death of her husband, Henry. I hoped she would take some of my desserts on consignment. She had nothing to lose if they didn't sell, and I knew they would sell.

I had brought iced oatmeal raisin cookies, apple pie, carrot cake, blueberry sour cream pie, and orange chocolate cheesecake. I packed each one carefully to keep them fresh and then put them into individual shopping bags to keep them from squishing one another.

When we got to the restaurant, we struggled to carry them into the inside, but we somehow managed it.

"Eileen, is Cynthia around?" I asked the waitress when she passed us.

She stopped and turned around. "Ayup, she's in the office. You can go back, Allie. She don't mind," she said in between smacking her gum.

"Come on," I said, leading Lucy back. No one knew it, but Lucy and I had broken into the restaurant one night, trying to look for clues to Henry Hoffer's murder. We don't normally resort to crime, but I was a suspect, and no way was I taking the fall for the real murderer.

We passed the kitchen on our way back and the cook, Charles Allen, stopped chopping onions to look at me. I stopped in my tracks and narrowed my eyes at him. He had squealed on me and told Alec I had argued with Henry Hoffer the night before he was murdered. This was before Alec and I were dating, and I felt like I had been pushed up the list of suspects to the number one position because of Charles. I wasn't over it yet. Someday I'd pay him back.

Charles shook his head at me and went back to chopping onions.

"Come on, Allie, these are getting heavy," Lucy whined from behind me.

"Yeah, yeah," I said and headed to the office. I knocked on the open door.

"Hi, Allie," Cynthia said, looking up from her laptop. "This is a surprise."

I smiled. Henry had still been using a paper ledger, and it was nice to see Cynthia had made major progress into the twenty-first century.

"Hi, Cynthia. I know this is kind of a surprise, but I was wondering if you had time for a delicious snack? Maybe a couple?" I asked. I stepped into the office and set my bags on the desk. Lucy followed suit. The desk was a nice addition. Henry had attached a piece of plywood to the wall as a desk. I took this as a good sign that Cynthia wasn't afraid to part with a little money, and that was good news for me.

"A couple?" Cynthia asked, eyeing the bags.

"A few," I said, and began taking the baked goods from the bags.

Cynthia's eyes got big as I uncovered each item. The scent of oranges and sugar began filling the small office, and if Cynthia hadn't been hungry before we got there, she was now.

"To what do I owe this pleasure?" Cynthia asked, eyeing the orange chocolate cheesecake.

I liked Cynthia. We had met after Henry's death, and she seemed like a nice person. She looked a little older than I was, and her hair was a striking black color that caught glints of light from the fluorescent bulb overhead.

I took a deep breath and gathered my courage. "Cynthia, I was thinking about a business proposition," I said. "And a sampling of these lovely desserts will help explain that proposition. May I go and get some plates from the kitchen?"

"Of course," she said, and I trotted back to the kitchen. I stopped in the doorway and closed my eyes, willing my mind not to see the image of Henry Hoffer, dead on the floor with a knife stuck in his chest. That was something I didn't need to see again.

I forced myself to move forward. "Charles, I need three dessert plates, three forks, and a pie server. Please," I said.

Charles narrowed his eyes at me. "What for?"

"Now, Charles, don't take that tone with me. I'm serving your boss some dessert. You don't want to keep her waiting, do you?" I said sweetly.

"We have dessert here," he said. "I make chocolate cake almost every day."

"Almost every day?" I asked. "I bet your customers are excited about that when they happen to order it on the second or third day after you baked it, don't you?"

He snorted. "You think you're so high and mighty. Just because you can bake tasty desserts. If you had my budget and had to use margarine, I bet that would bring you down a peg or two."

"Nonsense. I know my desserts are high and mighty, but I'm not. And at least you're no longer buying those horrid frozen pies from Shaw's Market. I have to give you props on that."

"There wasn't anything wrong with those pies. They were fine," he said, going back to chopping his onions.

"Charles. The plates," I said. If I stood there much longer, I was going to reek of onions, and I didn't want Cynthia smelling onions when she tried that decadent cheesecake.

Charles slammed down the knife he had been using and gathered up what I had requested.

"Thank you," I called as I hurried back to the office.

"Here we are," I said, setting the plates on the desk. "Which would you like to try first?"

"They all look so good. I just couldn't wait. I already sampled the cookies, and they are so moist, I can hardly believe it!" she said.

"Thank you. Wait until you try the orange chocolate cheesecake," I said. "Would you like to try that first?"

"That sounds wonderful," Cynthia said, nodding.

"I want some of that," Lucy said. "Cheesecake is one of my favorites."

I gave her a look. We were here to sell my goods, not sample them. I cut Cynthia a small piece of the cheesecake and then cut a sliver for Lucy.

Cynthia took a forkful of cheesecake, making sure to get some chocolate ganache on her fork and put it in her mouth. She closed her eyes and slowly chewed. "Oh, my. This is so good," she said when she had swallowed. "It's creamy and orangey, and yet not overwhelmingly orangey. The chocolate really sets the orange flavor off." She took another bite and closed her eyes again, savoring the flavor.

"I worked on it for a while," I said. "I love the flavor of orange and chocolate together. It feels so fresh, yet decadent," I said and cut a piece of the apple pie for her. "Now, try this apple pie. It's my grandmama's recipe. She taught me everything I know about baking."

"Well, she knew a lot about baking, then," she said. "But tell me, Allie, why are you bringing these lovely desserts for me to try?"

"Well, here's the thing," I began and glanced at Lucy for support. I knew my baked goods were good, but selling myself in a business setting was hard for me. Lucy nodded her encouragement. "As you know, I had my blog on grief. And it seemed, after a while, that I needed to move on because it felt a little like I was reliving the whole grief process over and over as I wrote about it each week. So I ended the blog. And I'm thinking about starting a new blog. One on baking. And I need somewhere to try out the desserts I'm making, and I wondered if maybe you might like to sell some of my desserts on a consignment basis."

"Consignment?" she asked, sitting back in her chair.

"That's right. If the desserts don't sell, then that's on me. If they do sell, you get a commission."

"What kind of commission?" she asked, licking her fork. "This is so good."

"Let me get you some carrot cake," I said, taking her plate from her. I wanted her to try several items. "We can negotiate the commission. And I can bring in some kind of display case for them."

"Oh, and maybe you could get a dessert cart, and the waitresses could push the desserts around so people could look at everything," Lucy said. "You know, once they lay eyes on your desserts, people are going to have to buy them."

"That's a good idea," I said, nodding at Lucy. I was glad I had brought her along. She was always quick with the ideas.

I looked at Cynthia as she dug into the apple pie.

"The crust on this apple pie is so flaky," she exclaimed. Then she looked up at me. "You might have a good idea here. Maybe even great. I wouldn't lose anything if they didn't sell. But if they do, and I'm sure they will, and word of mouth spreads about your desserts being served here, it will bring in more business. But I need exclusivity. You can't sell your baked goods anywhere else."

"I wouldn't dare," I said. "So, is it a deal?"

Cynthia looked me in the eye. "It's a deal. Commission to be negotiated."

"Absolutely," I said. Cynthia was a keen businesswoman. Her late husband Henry had only been a so-so businessman. He had been cheap and cut corners. Cynthia knew a good business deal when she saw it, and she wasn't afraid to act on it. I liked that.

Chapter Ten

CYNTHIA WAS SOLD ON my desserts after tasting the orange chocolate cheesecake, and we hadn't touched the blueberry sour cream pie. After leaving the apple pie, oatmeal raisin cookies, and cheesecake for Cynthia, we put carrot cake and blueberry sour cream pie into the trunk of my car, and I got behind the wheel. I turned and looked at Lucy and squealed. "We did it!"

Lucy laid her head back on the headrest of the seat and laughed. "You did it! You are about to embark on a new career!"

We laughed until we ran out of steam, and then we sat for a few minutes. "I'm going to start a new chapter of my life," I said with satisfaction.

"I'm so proud of you. You've been through a lot these past few years, and you just keep going. Good work, you," Lucy said, patting my hand.

I smiled at her. "I'm so glad I've had you by my side to see me through it all."

"There's no place I'd rather be," she said. "And now that we've eaten far more sugar than we ought to, and spread it on pretty thickly here in the car, too, how about a nice coffee? It's cold, and I need something to chase that sugar down."

"You got it," I said and giggled. I had done it. I had convinced Cynthia to sell my baked goods. I wasn't sure if that or the blog would be the proverbial icing on the cake for my new career. I had intended the blog to be the main show, but maybe putting desserts on consignment at Henry's would be the main show.

The sky got darker as we drove to the Cup and Bean coffee shop, and I wondered if it was going to snow again. Alec would want his snow for snow cream, and I hoped I could get home in time to put a bucket out because I was not going out into the woods to try to get some. I had had enough of that.

The Cup and Bean had the best coffee in town, and the parking lot was more crowded than usual when we got there. I hugged my coat close to my body as we crossed the parking lot. The warmth of the building felt heavenly as we stepped through the door.

"Mmm," Lucy said, inhaling deeply. "Mama needs a vanilla latte."

"Me too," I said, and we got in line. There were four people ahead of us, and I recognized the girl in front of me. It was Laura Linney, one of Jennifer's friends.

"Hi, Laura," I said.

She turned around. "Hey, Allie, how are you? How's Jennifer? I haven't heard from her in nearly a month. We have got to get together, and soon!"

"We're both great. She's here quite a bit since her school isn't far away. You should come to dinner one night," I said. Laura was a sweet girl. When she had come to spend the night during her high school years, I could breathe a sigh of relief because I wouldn't constantly have to monitor what she and Jennifer were doing. She was just a good girl. Don't get me started on her cousin Dawn.

"I'd love to," she said. "I'll have to give Jennifer a call so I know when she's in town again."

For a few seconds, I wondered if I should bring up Iris Rose's murder. I glanced around to see who was close enough to overhear our conversation.

"Laura, did you hear what happened to Iris Rose? Wasn't she your second grade teacher?" I asked. I figured I might as well see if she knew anything.

"I did hear," she said, nodding. "What a tragedy. I can't imagine who would want to hurt poor Mrs. Rose. She was one of my favorite teachers."

"Jennifer's too," I agreed. "I just can't imagine who would do that to her."

"You know, I ran into her a couple of months ago, and she didn't seem herself," she said as we stepped forward a couple of feet in line.

"Oh? How so?"

"I don't know. Just really down. I asked her how she was, but then she perked up. I just kind of felt like she didn't want to talk about it, so I didn't press her," she said.

"I don't blame you. Some people are private that way," I said, nodding.

"Well, I'll see you soon, Allie," she said as her turn to order came.

I looked at Lucy. "She wasn't happy."

"Being married to a cheater can make you unhappy," she said.

"And having a crazy, controlling mother that butts into your marriage isn't any fun, either," I pointed out.

"No, it's not. Having to look at your husband's lover every day stinks, too," she said.

We stepped forward and placed our coffee orders, and then looked for a table in the crowded room. When I saw Mr. Winters in the corner with his newspaper, I steered Lucy over to his table.

"May we sit with you, Mr. Winters?"

He looked up from his paper and nodded. "What do you ladies need to know?" he asked.

Lucy and I looked at each other, then back to him. He was onto us. "Mr. Winters, have you heard anything about Iris Rose?"

"Iris Rose? She was murdered," he said confidently.

"Yes, we know that. But have you heard anything about the murder?" I tried to keep my voice low so no one would overhear, and we took a seat at his table.

He thought for a few moments. "No, can't say as I have."

That was disappointing. Mr. Winters was the best source of gossip in town. Gossip might be wrong, but it could sometimes get you answers.

"Oh wait, you know, I seem to recall that she and her mother didn't get along very well," he said thoughtfully.

"We had heard that," I said and sat back in my seat, stirring my latte. There had to be more information out there somewhere. Iris had a pristine reputation, and while it was most likely accurate, someone out there didn't like her, and there had to be a reason for it.

"And her mother lost custody of her when she was nine," he said, and then went back to reading his paper.

"Wait. What?" I asked. "How do you know that? And why did she lose custody?"

He closed his newspaper and folded it over. "Hilda Bixby liked to drink. She liked it so much that she preferred it to being a mother. I think it's probably more accurate to say that Hilda didn't lose custody of her daughter but gave it up voluntarily."

My mouth dropped open. What mother would do such a thing? I looked at Lucy. She stared back at me, wide-eyed.

"Are you sure?" I asked him.

He nodded. "I remember because my brother-in-law had a fling with her about that time. She lived a wild life, that one did. She also told him she wished Iris had never been born. The girl slowed her down."

"She wished Iris had never been born? What a horrible thing to say about your own child," I said.

"Did she ever get her back?" Lucy asked.

"Yes, she gave up the drinking and running around and convinced a judge to give her back when Iris was fourteen. Iris hated to go back to her. She had been living with her grandmother and was happy as could be. It was her first year of high school, and she had to change schools when her mother brought her back to Sandy Harbor," Mr. Winters said, nodding.

"I'd be unhappy too if my mother had given me up and then wanted me back when I had already found my own happiness," I said.

"Why did she want her back if she said she wished Iris had never been born?" Lucy asked. "It doesn't seem like she would have such a complete turnaround like that."

He shrugged. "Who knows? Maybe once she was sober, the guilt set in. It's hard to say."

It was a lot to absorb. It flew in the face of everything I believed as a mother, and I wasn't sure what to make of it. I wasn't so naïve as to think it didn't happen all the time in this world. It just wasn't something I could do.

I took a sip of my cooling latte and considered whether I was wrong about my assessment of Hilda Bixby. Maybe she *was* capable of murdering her only daughter. Maybe she still resented her daughter slowing her down, and when she couldn't control Iris like she wanted, she killed her. Richard Rose said she would go into rages. Maybe when she went down to the school to help Iris, she had lost her temper over something. I might have been grasping at straws, but it seemed more apparent that Hilda might have killed Iris.

I signaled to Lucy, and we stood up.

"Thank you, Mr. Winters. If you think of anything else, will you call me?" I asked.

"Well, I would if I had your phone number," he said, cocking his head as if to say I was a dummy.

"Of course," I said and dug through my purse. I found a business card for my grief blog and handed it to him. I was going to have to make some up for my soon-to-be baking blog. "It's on there."

He looked the card over. "A grief blog?" he asked questioningly.

I nodded. "Soon to be a baking blog," I said and left him looking befuddled.

"Let's go, we have work to do," I whispered to Lucy as we headed for the door.

Chapter Eleven

"SO, WHERE ARE WE HEADED?" Lucy asked when we got into the car.

I turned toward her. "I think we should pay Hilda Bixby a visit. Maybe take her a pie as a token of our sympathies. I just think there has to be more there, somewhere."

"Do you think she killed Iris? And then, what? Took her out to the woods?" she asked.

"Maybe. But Hilda isn't a large woman. I'm not sure she could have carried her from a murder site and then dragged her out into the woods and buried her. That's a lot of physical work. Maybe she took her out into the woods and killed her there. That would be easier."

"Were there footprints in the snow where Iris was found?" she asked. "Maybe she had someone help her?"

I shook my head. "No. It had snowed the night before we found her. The snow would have covered any prints."

"Right," she said, thinking. "It's possible she had help. Oh, I know, maybe Iris's mother and her husband plotted together and killed her and took her out there."

"Not likely," I said. "Richard Rose and Hilda hate each other. Even if it benefited the two of them, I highly doubt they could have cooperated long enough to kill her and get her buried in the snow. And I can't imagine how they both would benefit."

"Maybe they were in love with each other?" she said starting to get excited.

"Lucy. I just said that they hated each other," I said.

"Maybe there was insurance money?" she suggested.

"That's something Alec needs to check into," I said.

"Well, let's go see Hilda and see what she has to say," she said, buckling her seat belt.

WE CLIMBED THE STEPS up to Hilda's apartment over the garage, looking over our shoulders to make sure Richard wasn't watching. I didn't see a car in the driveway, so I thought he must be gone somewhere. I had read in the newspaper that Iris's funeral was the following day. I didn't think Alec and I would show up for it since we hadn't known her well.

"Wow, Hilda must be in good shape to climb these every day," Lucy panted. Her foot slipped, and she grabbed tighter to the railing. "Whoa."

"Be careful," I said, looking over my shoulder. "The snow doesn't help. I'd have taken a tumble down them by now if I wasn't as athletic as I am."

I stood with my hand poised to knock on the door and it flew open. "Oh!" I nearly squealed. "Hello, Hilda, I-we were in the neighborhood and we thought we'd stop by."

Hilda squinted her eyes and leaned past me to get a look at Lucy.

"This is my friend Lucy Gray. We, uh, brought you a pie," I said indicating the shopping bag I had on my arm. I had one hand on the landing railing and suddenly felt a little queasy at the stair height. I wasn't good with heights, and this garage apartment suddenly seemed terribly high.

"Hi," Lucy said, still clutching the railing. "Oh say, don't I know you? You worked at the library for a while, didn't you? And the bank?"

Lucy was an avid reader and user of the public library, but I had no idea Hilda had ever worked there.

Hilda took a step back. "I've worked in both places. You like John Grisham, don't you?"

"Wow, you have quite the memory," Lucy said. "It's been years since you've worked there, hasn't it?"

"It has," Hilda agreed. She still had a very somber look on her face, and I wasn't sure she would let us in. Then she suddenly took another step back and held the door open. "Why don't you come in?"

We followed her into the apartment. "I love what you've done with this place," Lucy said, following me in. "And I'm so sorry about your daughter. What a terrible tragedy."

"Thank you," Hilda said. "I still can't believe it's true. I suppose I won't until I actually see her. The viewing is this evening."

"I'm so sorry," I said. My heart went out to her, regardless of whether what Mr. Winter's said was true or not. "I was baking yesterday, and I made you a blueberry sour cream pie, Hilda. Would you like me to cut a piece for you?"

She looked at me, surprised, and then her eyes went to the shopping bag I held.

"Well, I suppose a little wouldn't hurt. I do love blueberries," she said.

"I'm so glad," I said and headed to her little kitchenette. "If you don't mind, I'll help myself with finding the dishes?"

"Oh, sure," she said absently. "Have you read Grisham's latest?" she said to Lucy, motioning toward one of the loveseats.

"I haven't. The library hasn't gotten it in yet. But I placed a request for it to come from the Bangor library. Is it good?" Lucy asked enthusiastically.

"I don't think it's one of his best," she said. "But it's not his worst, either."

I opened a cupboard and found her dishes. The plates were a plain white Corelle. I took out three dessert plates and three coffee cups. Pie and coffee was the way to anyone's heart, not to mention thoughts. It was easier for people to open up over good food. A small four-cup coffee maker sat on the corner of the countertop beside a white ceramic canister of coffee. It was the perfect size for such a small kitchen. I quickly got a pot of coffee brewing and then turned to the pie.

It smelled wonderful. I had made a crumb topping, and blueberry juice had bubbled up around the edges during baking. I made a mental note to use blueberries more often. They were a superfood and tasted great in just about everything.

Lucy and Hilda discussed books as the coffee brewed. I could have gotten in on the discussion since I love books too, but Lucy was doing an excellent job of getting Hilda to loosen up.

I found a serving tray and poured three cups of coffee and put them on the tray along with sugar and the cream I found in the refrigerator. Hilda didn't seem to mind me making myself at home. I put three pieces of pie on the tray and headed to the living room.

"Here we are," I said, setting the tray on the coffee table and taking a seat next to Lucy.

"Oh, that pie looks lovely," Hilda said, reaching for a cup of coffee and fixing it to her liking.

"Thank you, I think it's one of my better pies," I said, trying to sound humble. Where my pies are concerned, humble is a hard one for me.

"I've tried a piece of your cherry pie before," she said, reaching for a piece of pie.

"Oh? When did you try that?" I asked, stirring my coffee.

"At the Halloween bazaar. I have to say, it was one of the best pieces of cherry pie I've ever eaten," she said.

"Oh, thank you. That's sweet of you to say," I said. It always made me feel good when someone complimented my baking, and I didn't think Hilda was one to give idle compliments.

"Allie is going to sell her pies and desserts at Henry's Home Cooking Restaurant," Lucy said, tasting a piece of the pie. "Mmm, Allie, this is so good."

"How wonderful. I guess I know where to go whenever I need something sweet," Hilda said.

"Thank you, ladies," I said. "It's good to hear that someone enjoys my cooking. Hilda, how are you doing? This has got to be so hard on you."

She sighed heavily, and her eyes welled up with tears. "It is. As a mother, you go over all the things you did or didn't do and the things you wish you could have changed."

"I can imagine," I said. It was unthinkable that a child would die before a parent. "I have a blog on grief. I'm no longer updating it, but there are eight years' worth of articles on there. You might find it helpful." I handed her a business card with the web address on it.

She looked at it. "I'm not big on the Internet, but I'll try to take a look," she said.

"I know some people aren't really into the Internet, but I think it's good to have help to get through this sort of thing. Have you considered counseling?"

She sighed. "You know what would help me get through this?" she asked.

"What would that be?" I asked, feeling like I wouldn't like the answer.

"It would be to see the murderer in the front house thrown in jail for the rest of his life," she said, pointing at Richard's house.

"Oh, well, I know they're working on figuring out who the murderer is," I stammered.

"I already know who it is," she said. Anger was creeping into her voice, and I wondered if we were going to see the rage Richard had spoken of.

I nodded my head. "I'm sure the police will find the guilty person and—"

"I *know* who the guilty person is!" she said, cutting me off. Things were going from nice and friendly to not so friendly.

"I think what Allie is trying to say is, the police need to follow certain procedures so they can make the arrest and make it stick," Lucy interjected.

Hilda took a deep breath. "I suppose that's necessary. But I do know who did it."

"What makes you know this?" Lucy asked gently.

"I told her already," she said, nodding toward me. "That worthless husband of Iris's had an affair on her with a much younger woman. He wanted Iris gone so he could be with her. He didn't want a messy divorce. No, that would have been too easy. He's heartless."

Lucy nodded. "You spoke about regrets. What would you have changed?" she asked. She was trying to change the subject, but it felt like too fast of a switch, and I hoped it didn't backfire on her.

Hilda sat up straight. "I would have been a better mother. I—I would have spent more time with her when she was a child. I loved her. I don't care what anyone says."

I nodded. "Raising a child is hard," I encouraged. "All parents have regrets."

"I put her into foster care," she suddenly said. "I did it, it's true. But I was a different person back then. And my mother got custody, so it's not like it was a stranger that I had given her over to." Her voice cracked on the last part. "The truth was, my mother was a terrible mother when I was young, and I handed my daughter over to her. But I do have to admit that she was much better with Iris. I guess she had matured by the time Iris came into her life."

"I'm so sorry," I said. There didn't seem to be anything else I could say at that point.

"I hated her," she spat out, looking at me. "There were days I absolutely hated my daughter. I don't know why." She took a deep breath. "She was so nice and sweet and spineless and weak, and it irritated me. There. There it is. Is that what you came for?" Bitterness laced each word as she spoke it.

I stared at her, wide-eyed. I had no idea what to say to this. I looked at Lucy for help.

"Hilda, no one knows what a person has walked through in their life. They can judge and think they know it all, but the truth is, the rest of us are looking in through a small window into another person's life. We don't know. No one does. But you tried to do better, and that's all you could do," Lucy said quietly.

Hilda turned to Lucy, and her face softened a little. "I think I need to be alone now."

Chapter Twelve

"I'M TIRED. I NEED MORE sleep," I said as Alec put a plate of scrambled eggs in front of me. "But thanks for making breakfast."

"You need to run more. That will give you more energy," he replied, sitting across from me.

I narrowed my eyes at him. "Are you serious? I'm running forty miles a week."

"Ah. Well, I guess it's something else," he said. A small smile played on his lips.

"You know, you're not as serious as I thought you were when we first met," I said, and took a drink of my coffee.

He chuckled. "I've changed? Well, I'd be boring if I were as serious as you first thought."

"Have you heard anything new about Iris's murder?" I asked.

"Her neck was broken," he said, taking a bite of eggs.

"Really? So it could have been an accident? Maybe she slipped on ice," I said, and then realized that was dumb.

"Well, it could be, except that she didn't bury herself," he said with a smirk.

"What if she slipped and fell out there and broke her neck and the snow-covered her body?" I asked. I just wanted to cover all the angles.

"Possible, but not probable. It was too cold to be out there on foot, and there wasn't anything beneath her but dirt and snow. It really wasn't that slippery," he answered.

"She could have been out there, going for a walk," I pointed out. "Maybe she spent a lot of time out in the woods and was used to the cold. Therefore, she wouldn't need heavier shoes and clothes."

"But neither her husband nor her mother mentioned it, therefore you're just being silly."

"And there wasn't a car," I said.

"Right."

I sighed. "I'm too tired this morning to figure out what happened to her. My brain isn't working."

"I'm not going to touch that one," he wisely said.

"Well," I began, not looking at him. "I did learn something."

"Uh oh. What might that be?" he asked suspiciously.

I looked him in the eye. "I'm helping you, whether you like it or not, so you may as well be happy about it."

He chuckled again. "That's what I'm afraid of. You're helping me whether I like it or not."

I decided to ignore that comment. "It seems Hilda had a drinking problem in her younger years and she is never going to be voted mother of the year."

"Well, that would apply to many mothers, and fathers as well. But I'm assuming since she was living in the apartment over Iris's garage, that they mended their past."

"That's what Hilda says. But Mr. Winters said that Hilda said she wished Iris was never born and that she voluntarily gave up custody, only to take it back about five years later," I said.

"Wait, that's what Hilda said? You went to talk to Hilda after we talked to her the first time?" he asked, fork poised mid-air.

I had hoped he would miss that part, but he was, after all, an ace detective. "I brought her a pie. Food always makes the hurt easier to bear."

"Listen, Allie, I appreciate the help. Sometimes. But I don't think you should go to a possible suspect's house and interview them by yourself. I've told you this before. You never know when you might push them too far," he said. He gave me a hard look and put his fork down on his plate.

"I wasn't alone. I brought Lucy," I said, and filled my mouth with egg and toast to keep from saying anything else.

He sighed. "I wonder why that doesn't make me feel better?"

I chewed and swallowed quickly. "Look, I know it's not the ideal situation, but Richard is right. She does have anger issues—"

"And I know how you have issues with people with anger issues, but it doesn't mean a thing," he said, cutting me off.

I sighed. "Will you let me finish? She admitted to making mistakes. Giving up custody was a big one for her, and she admits it. And why are you skipping over the fact that she said she wished Iris was never born?"

"So?" he said, shrugging her shoulders. "It doesn't seem unusual that a parent would regret giving up custody. It wouldn't surprise me if a desperate parent would admit to wishing they'd never had their child. It would have made things easier if they hadn't, and Hilda knew she made a mistake and tried to make it right by taking her daughter back."

"Giving up custody is something most people wouldn't do in the first place," I said. "It was weird though. It seemed like she knew why we were there, and she told us anyway. Maybe I'm wrong, but I think there's something there."

"Okay, duly noted. I'll write it down, and we'll see what happens," he said.

"That's all I'm asking," I answered.

"Will it do any good for me to ask you not to talk to people without me?" he asked.

I smiled at him. "Probably not. What is all that?" I asked, pointing to a stack of papers on the table next to him.

"That is my application for a PI license with the great state of Maine."

"Really? All that?" I asked. It would have taken me weeks to assemble all that he had in the stack.

"Ayup," he said in his best Maine accent. "Apparently they don't hand these licenses out to just anyone. I still need to take a test once they approve all this," he said, pulling the stack toward himself. "There are transcripts from the police academy, my high school diploma, birth certificate, oh, and a release to do a psychiatric check. Just to mention a few."

"Wow, sounds like fun. I hope you pass the inspection. Especially that psychiatric check."

"We can only hope," he said. "Can I use your scanner to send it all in?"

"Sure you can," I said.

"And let's go take another look at the place we found the body, shall we?"

"Really?" I asked. "That sounds like fun."

"We can get some snow for snow cream."

"No. Way."

ALEC AND I WALKED AROUND the area where we had found Iris. There hadn't been much new snow, and what was there had begun to melt, in spite of the cold temperatures. I had worn rugged boots and a double layer of socks, so at least I was warmer this time.

"What do you think we're going to find?" I asked him.

"I don't know. I was just wondering if the melting snow would reveal anything new," he said, squatting down to get a better look at the place Iris had laid. He reached out a gloved hand and dug up some of the icy snow.

"Shouldn't the police have found all there was to find?" I asked.

"Yes, they should have. But it's hard to find clues when the ground is frozen and covered in snow," he said. "Something might have been left behind."

I walked around the area, searching the ground for anything. The top layer of snow was more of an ice crust caused by melting snow and the temperatures dropping and re-freezing the snow at night. I wondered if the crime had been committed by someone who knew what they were doing and had cleaned up after themselves, or if it was an amateur that had left clues behind. My bet was on this being a crime of passion. Done in anger. If I was right, there would be clues somewhere.

Alec had a small hand-held garden shovel used to transplant plants. He was digging with more intention, and I went over to him. "Did you find something?"

"Yeah. A set of keys," he said, wiggling them free of the ice.

"Huh. Maybe they fell out of Iris's pocket?"

"Maybe," he said and continued digging in the area he had found the keys.

"What is that?" I asked, squatting down next to him.

"A ring," he said, holding it up.

"Iris's wedding rings," I said. The ring was yellow gold with a heart-shaped diamond and three tiny diamonds on each side. It had been soldered to a plain gold wedding band.

"Let's see if there are any other treasures," he said, continuing to dig.

The wedding ring made me sad. It was such a personal item. "I thought Iris had a wedding ring on her hand when we found her?"

He looked at me. "Are you sure?"

"I think so," I said, trying to remember her hands.

"That's another mystery to solve then."

Chapter Thirteen

I WASN'T GOING TO DO it. But then I decided I had to do it. I think funerals should be private affairs with only the closest of loved ones. Death is an intimate thing, something one goes through alone. I've always felt the funeral should be an intimate affair as well, with only close loved ones. But they're not.

My late husband's funeral was attended by scads of people I didn't even know. Work colleagues, college friends, old high school buddies, and everyone in between. And because funerals are not private, intimate affairs, I decided I could attend Iris's funeral. After all, she had been my daughter's second grade teacher and well-beloved by said daughter.

So without any further ado, I had put on my funeral dress and black pumps and was headed to the funeral home. I opened my front door and screamed.

"Hey!" Alec exclaimed, wide-eyed.

"Oh!" I said, staring back at him.

"What's wrong?" he asked with concern in his voice.

"Nothing. You startled me."

He looked me up and down. "You look very nice. Are you going somewhere?" he asked with one eyebrow cocked.

I gave him a lopsided smile. "You look nice, too. Are you going somewhere?" He was dressed in a casual black suit. One appropriate for small-town funerals.

"I asked you first," he said.

"I'm going to a funeral," I said and pushed past him, pulling my front door closed behind me.

He sighed loudly. "Now, how did I know that? And why didn't you tell me?" he said to my back.

"Why didn't you tell me you were going?" I asked, unlocking my car door. "How did you get here?"

"My neighbor was headed this direction, so he dropped me off. I was going to ask you to borrow your car. I really need to get one of my own."

"Well, come on then, before I leave you behind," I said, getting into my car and shutting the door.

He trotted over to the passenger side and got in. "Going my way?"

"You're so cute," I said and started the car and backed out of my driveway. "So who do you think will be at the funeral? Jennifer wanted to go, but she has a test that she couldn't get out of."

"Seeing as how it's Sandy Harbor, I'd say just about everyone will be there," he said.

"I agree. But it's mostly because Iris was a well-liked schoolteacher. You can't get any more popular than that in a small town."

"That's true," he said.

THE PARKING LOT OF the funeral home was packed. Cars lined the curb around it and filled the parking lot across the street at the medical office complex. I always thought it was convenient having a funeral home across the street from the doctor's offices. You never know when something might go wrong.

I parked the car three blocks away and took Alec's arm as we walked up to the funeral home.

"Catch me if I slip on these sidewalks," I said to Alec. We had had a freeze overnight, and there were patches of ice on the sidewalk.

"I will if you'll catch me," he said.

"Uh, I'm not so sure about that. You're a lot bigger than I am," I said as my foot slipped out from under me. Alec caught me before disaster struck.

"Like that?" he asked with a grin.

"Just like that," I said.

Once inside, we found a seat in the back. If many more people showed up, it was going to be standing room only. I nudged Alec when I spotted Josh Stine sitting near the middle. He kept dabbing at his eyes with a tissue. I turned to Alec, and he shrugged. Lots of people were going to miss Iris.

I nudged him again when I spotted Janice. He turned toward the other side of the room and nodded slowly. I had to wonder why she was there. Had she and Iris made up after the affair was revealed? Or was she there for moral support for Richard? She sat next to three other women I recognized as elementary school teachers. If they were unaware of the affair, then it made sense that Janice would come if they asked. It would seem odd if she refused.

I leaned over to whisper to Alec. "I hope Hilda doesn't freak out when she sees Janice here."

Alec turned to me. "Oh, now that wouldn't be good." He sighed. "I wish people would think things through before attending funerals."

I stifled a laugh. "You better keep an eye on things."

Then I spotted Hilda as she staggered her way up the aisle toward the casket. It looked like Hilda had fallen off the wagon. We watched as she leaned over the thankfully closed casket and began sobbing.

"I'm so sorry, baby," she cried. "I'm so sorry."

We watched, unable to look away for nearly five uncomfortable minutes. "Maybe you should do something?" I whispered to Alec. I didn't want to see her open the casket and cry all over Iris.

"I'm not the funeral bouncer, you know," he said.

"I know, but someone needs to help her, just in case. You know?"

He sighed with resignation and got to his feet, making his way slowly down the aisle. I saw him whisper something to Hilda, and she turned to look at him, her face turning a darker shade of red. I instantly regretted sending him down there. I saw Alec's lips move, and Hilda seemed to take a deep breath. She nodded and took his arm, and they slowly made her way to the front pew. Hilda turned to him and nodded and sat down.

Alec made his way back to me and sat beside me. "Satisfied?"

"Very much so," I said. "You're such a gentleman."

"I try."

Richard sat on one end of the front pew, and Hilda sat on the other. A woman about Hilda's age and a man approached her and hugged her, then sat next to her. I wondered if they were Iris's aunt and uncle.

I glanced at my phone for the time and then turned the volume down in case it went off. We had another ten minutes until the service began, and so far everyone was behaving themselves.

A few people went to the casket and laid a hand on it or spoke to it, and it looked like things were going according to plan so far.

Then I saw Josh stand up and make his way to the aisle and up to the casket. His shoulders began to shake, and his head bowed. I looked at Alec.

"I'm not going up there," he said, looking at me.

I shrugged. I guess he couldn't rescue everyone.

A few seconds later and Josh was crying loudly. He slammed a fist into the top of the casket and laid his head down on top of it.

"Alec," I hissed.

"Oh, come on, Allie," he said, putting his head down. "I can't do this."

"Richard looks really uncomfortable," I whispered.

He looked to where Richard was squirming in his seat.

"Why can't people behave at funerals?" he asked.

"Why do you think Josh is that emotional?" I whispered.

Alec shrugged. "He was kind of wired that day we saw him. He's kind of nerdy. Maybe he's got some emotional problems."

"Are you going up there?" I whispered.

Alec put his head back and looked at the ceiling for a few moments. He sighed and stood up and made his way to Josh and whispered to him. Josh quieted down and then looked at Alec and nodded and then made his way back to his seat. Easy as that.

"What did you say to him?" I whispered when Alec sat down beside me.

"I told him she was in a better place now, and she would be watching over him," he said.

I slapped his arm. "You did not," I hissed.

He shrugged. "I did. What else do you tell someone like that? He isn't family, and to be reacting that way, he's got to be a little nutty."

THE SERVICE WENT OFF without a hitch, and if it hadn't been for Josh, it would have been completely uneventful. It was a relief, and I was glad when it was over. My heels were killing me, and I wanted to take them off.

"What did you think about Josh acting that way?" I asked Alec as I fastened my seatbelt. I had given him the car keys so I could kick my shoes off in the car. Wearing running shoes all day had made me unaccustomed to wearing high heels.

"I'm not sure what to think. I suppose he bears watching," Alec said.

"We need to talk to him. His behavior is highly suspicious, if you ask me," I said.

"You think everyone's suspicious," he said.

"Oh, come on," I said. "You aren't at all suspicious of him?"

"Actually, I am. And yes, we should talk to him. Does that make you feel better?" he asked.

"Yes, very much so," I said and headed toward home. "We also need to get with Sam at the police department and see where the investigation is going."

"Oh, can't wait to do that," he said.

"And I need to get home and get some baking done. I'm thinking a cheesecake of some kind. Maybe I'll start with two different desserts per day to take to Henry's. What do you think?"

"I think two a day is a good amount. Not too overwhelming," he said. "And you'll make enough for me to sample, right?"

"I think you need to keep an eye on your diet. You have a marathon to run in a few months."

We were stopped at a signal light, and he turned to look at me.

"Light's green," I said.

Chapter Fourteen

"I COMPLETELY FORGOT to ask, how was the funeral?" Lucy asked me. She was leaning against my kitchen counter sampling my oatmeal raisin cookies. I was still working on the recipe and had added extra nutmeg to them. It made the flavor pop.

"Oh, you know. It was a funeral. Not much to tell," I said, sitting down at my kitchen table. I'd been on my feet all morning baking, and I was pooped.

"You should have told me you were going. I enjoy a good funeral," she said, picking up another cookie. Her blond hair was escaping the thick knit cap she was still wearing. The kitchen was warm from baking, and she was making me sweat just looking at that hat.

"Why don't you take that hat off? Aren't you hot with it on?" I asked, leaning back in my chair.

"I can't. I didn't brush my hair this morning. Were there a lot of people there?" she asked.

"Since when is brushing your hair optional if you're going out?" I asked. I mean, who did that? As an adult, I mean?

"Since I have a hat to hide it under. Answer me. Was there anyone interesting there?" she asked.

"Alec and I were there. We're interesting. And yes, there were a lot of people. She was a good teacher, and people really liked her. It's such a shame. Oh, do you know a Josh Stine by chance?"

Her forehead scrunched up in thought. "Oh, you know, I think Melanie Stine is his mom. She works at Walmart. But I don't think I know him. Why?"

"When we went to the school to talk to Janice Cross, he was there. He brought roses to Iris's classroom. He was also at the funeral, and he got very emotional," I told her.

"Really? Why would he bring her roses? Did he know she was dead or did he think he was bringing them for her, and she would be there to accept them from him?" she asked and came and sat at the table next to me.

"Yeah, he knew she was dead. He was a former student, and I guess it made him feel good to bring the roses to her classroom," I said with a shrug. "It makes some people feel good to bring flowers to the place they associate with the deceased person the most."

"Do you suspect him? That's it, isn't it?" she asked, eyeing me.

"Alec says I suspect everyone," I said and got up to get myself a cookie.

"You do. Do you want to interrogate him?"

"I'd like to talk to his mom," I said. "I bet she could give us some insight into him. Wait. She works at Walmart? He said he left college to take care of her because she was sick."

"If she's sick, it must be something recent. I think I saw her about a month ago, and she seemed fine," she said.

"Hmm," I said thoughtfully.

"I know that look. Let's go," Lucy said, getting to her feet.

WALMART WASN'T NEARLY as busy as I thought it would be when we got there. That was good. We'd have more of a chance to get Melanie Stine alone.

"What department?" I asked Lucy as we walked in.

"She's a checker," she said, and we walked down the line of cash registers, looking for her. I had no idea what she looked like, but there were only four young, college-age girls on the registers, so I knew she wasn't there.

"Maybe it's her day off," I said.

Lucy sighed. "Maybe she's around. Let's go for a walk."

We headed toward clothing and went through each section, looking around displays and down each aisle. No Melanie.

"I bet she's off today," I said.

"Maybe. Let's look in another department."

We wandered around the entire store, and all we had to show for it was my feet hurting more than they had when we started.

"I guess we better go," I said. I was tired and ready to put my feet up. "Do you have her number? Maybe you can call her?"

"No, we're more acquaintances than anything," she said. "I used to see her at my therapist's office, and we struck up a conversation, and then I saw her working here. She's a nice person."

"Wait, you have a therapist?" I asked. It was the first I'd heard of it.

"Not for a few years," she said, looking at me. "What? It takes a lot to keep the crazy in, sometimes. Let's stop off in produce before we leave. I need to make a salad for dinner. Ed's on a new health kick."

"All right," I said, and we headed over.

The produce section was nicely taken care of, and although it wasn't as big as Shaw's Market's produce section, it was adequate. If I had to work at Walmart, I would want to work in produce. There weren't nearly as many pesky customers in this section.

"Hi, Melanie!" Lucy called out as we looked through the lettuces.

A woman with a green apron and holding a produce spray hose turned around. "Hi, Lucy," she said. "How are you?"

Melanie had short red curly hair and wore gold wire-rimmed glasses. She looked to be in her early fifties, and she had a big smile on her face.

"Are you in produce now?" Lucy asked. We crossed the distance between us to where Melanie was lightly spraying down a display of fresh berries. I made a mental note to get more blueberries.

"Yeah, I got a promotion," she said. "I love it!"

Lucy introduced us, and I let Lucy lead since I didn't know Melanie.

"So, Melanie, how have things been? I haven't seen you in here for a while, and I was hoping you weren't sick or anything," Lucy said with concern.

"Me? No, I'm healthy as a horse. I never get sick," she said and chuckled. "I eat a lot of vegetables."

"Oh, that's good to hear. I must have come in on your day off," Lucy said, giving me the eye. "So, how were your holidays? Did your son come to spend Christmas with you? You did tell me you had one son, right?"

At the mention of her son, Melanie stopped smiling. "He did come home. I think I'm going to try to get him in to see Dr. Stewart. I think maybe a little therapy might be good for him. I'm worried about him."

"Oh no," Lucy said. "What's wrong?"

I shook my head sympathetically.

She sighed and looked around. "He flunked out of school. He had wanted to go to Texas so badly, but he didn't like it when he got there. He just wasn't up to it. It's not that he isn't a good student, you know, but he's such a shy boy. It makes it hard for him to fit in. I told him to try to get into a distance learning program with the University of Maine."

"College can be difficult for a lot of kids," I said. "I have a daughter that's the sensitive sort, and she struggles sometimes. She stayed local for college so she could come home when she needed to. Maybe he could look into something close by?"

"Really? I should suggest that to him. What did you say your daughter's name was?" she asked.

"Jennifer," I replied without thinking.

"You know, maybe we should, you know, get them together? She's shy, he's shy. It could be a match made in heaven," she said, beaming.

"Oh," I said. I hadn't thought of that when I'd volunteered the information about Jennifer. I had only said it to gain her sympathy and get her to open up.

"I think that's a great idea," Lucy said, looking at me and giving me a wink.

Jennifer would kill me. And I was going to kill Lucy. Alec would have to bail one or both of us out of jail, but I was not letting Josh anywhere near my daughter.

"I'll certainly ask her, but you know, now that I think of it, I think she said she was seeing a new boy," I said with a big smile.

"Oh, of course," Melanie said. "I bet she's a cute girl if she looks anything like you. But if it doesn't work out, you'll keep my Josh in mind, won't you?"

Did she think the kid was applying for a job?

"Oh, of course," I said. "We better get going, Lucy. Ed's expecting that salad."

"Yeah, we better get going. It was nice to see you again, Melanie. And congratulations on the new position," Lucy said. "We'll be seeing you around."

"Yes, I'll be seeing you," Melanie said.

We picked up a bag of lettuce, a tomato, and some blueberries and headed for the checkout. "Thanks for volunteering Jennifer for her kid," I said. "I'm sure Jennifer will be thrilled."

Lucy giggled. "Stop it. I was just trying to gain her trust."

"Yeah, right."

"What did you think about what she said?" Lucy whispered as we waited in line.

"Josh is a liar and a social misfit. It doesn't give me a warm fuzzy feeling, that's for sure," I said.

We checked out and headed home.

Chapter Fifteen

"THIS IS PERFECT!" I said as Alec pulled the dessert display stand out of the shipping box.

"Yes, and apparently assembly is required," he said as he pulled out glass panels sandwiched between Styrofoam sheets.

"Oh, but you're so talented, it'll be easy for you," I said, looking over the instructions. The display stand was pricey, but it would be worth it. It had wheels, so Cynthia would be able to move it if need be.

We had temporarily taken over Cynthia's office for assembly purposes. Once Alec had all the parts laid out on the floor, he pulled out his toolbox. I didn't even know he owned one.

"You know what?" I asked as I studied the instructions.

"What?" he asked, picking up part of the cherry wood frame.

"I'm thinking I over-bought on this thing. If I'm only making two desserts a day, this thing's going to be nearly empty."

"Hmm," he said, holding his hand out for the instruction sheet. "I guess you can cut the pies and have pieces displayed on plates."

"I don't think they'll stay fresh. And I think plastic wrap will make them look too cafeteria-ish. I can't have that," I said.

"Bake two of each and space them out," he said absently. He pulled out a cordless screwdriver and began attaching one side of the frame to another.

"Maybe I can put something in the display case with them. Like for holiday months, I could put ornaments or decorations of some kind in it. Or teacups on saucers. Or something. I'm going to have to get with Lucy on this," I said.

"Well, you two have your work cut out for you," Cynthia said, poking her head in the open door.

"Hey, Cynthia, I'm thinking about bringing two of each dessert I make. Does that sound right to you?" I asked.

"Yeah. We can adjust the amounts once we see how many we sell. Weekends are busier, so you'll probably sell more then. Tuesdays are slower. It'll probably take a while to figure it out," she said. "I think it's a great idea though."

"I do too," I said. "I can hardly wait."

"You could always sell whole pies and cakes that people can take home," Alec said, studying the directions.

"That's a great idea," I said, brightening. "I knew I was keeping you around for a reason."

Cynthia laughed. "I'm going to leave you two alone so you can finish this job."

"Okay," I told her. "Alec, you're such a smart cookie."

"I know," he said, giving me a big smile.

"HEY, YANCEY," I SAID as Alec held the front door to the police station open for me, and I stepped inside.

"Hi, Allie, Alec. How are you two doing this morning?" he asked. Yancey was sitting at a desk covered in paperwork and rummaging through it.

"Great," Alec answered. "Is Sam around?" Alec had already brought the wedding rings and keys we found at the site where we found Iris's body down to the police station.

"Ayup, he's in his office. You can head on back," he said, pointing to the hallway.

"Thanks," I said. "I need to bring you some cookies, Yancey."

"That'd be much appreciated, Allie," he said as we passed his desk.

I didn't much care for the chief of police, Sam Bailey, but that was mostly because Alec didn't like him. I had gotten a little more information out of him as to the cause of the friction, but it wasn't much. It seemed Sam just resented having Alec foisted on him when he had been a detective. The feeling was mutual on Alec's part.

Alec knocked on Sam's closed door.

"Yeah?" he called.

"It's Alec Blanchard," he said, and he gave me a look.

I almost giggled. Sam knew who he was without him giving his last name.

"Come in," he called.

Alec opened the door for me.

"Hi Allie," Sam said. "I wasn't expecting you."

"Just consider me a surprise," I said and took a seat in front of his desk without asking.

Alec sat next to me. "Have you found out anything new?" he asked Sam.

"Not really. The only thing we know is what I've told you. That Iris Rose's neck was broken, and she had bruises and contusions on her body. Looks like she got into a fight with the killer," he said, picking up a file with Iris's name on it.

"What about Richard Rose and her mother, Hilda Bixby? Do you have anything on them?" I asked. I wondered if he had a different impression than I did. As far as I was concerned, either of them could have done it.

Sam made a face when I asked, then straightened up. "Not really. George spoke to both of them, and they seem to check out," he said.

"What about the rings and the keys we found out where her body was?" Alec asked.

"That was kind of odd. She had a wedding ring on her finger when she was found. We gave it to Richard, and he took it without a word. Then we showed him the rings you found, and he lit up like a Christmas tree. Said that was Iris's wedding set," he said, sitting back in his chair. "He confirmed the keys were his wife's."

"Wait, she had two wedding rings?" I asked.

He shrugged. "Richard said she was always losing the engagement ring, and when we gave him the plain band, he assumed it was hers. When he saw the other rings, he said he remembered she had them soldered together a couple of years ago so she wouldn't lose one of them. He said he had forgotten about it and just thought the engagement ring was at his house somewhere."

"So where did the extra ring come from?" I asked, glancing at Alec.

"We do not know."

"And why would the wedding rings be in the snow near her body and not on her finger?" I asked.

"I do not have an answer for that one, either," he said.

"Looks like we've got more investigating to do," Alec said. "Did the medical examiner say how he thought she got the bruises and contusions?"

He shook his head. "Like I said, I'm sure the killer must have hit her."

"I didn't look at her for long, but did she have any bruises on her face? I don't remember seeing any, and it seems like if the killer had beaten her up, he would have hit her in the face at least once," I pointed out.

He shook his head. Sam had a very laissez-faire attitude about the whole thing, and I didn't like it.

"What about what was in her hand when we found her? Her hand had frozen closed over it," Alec asked.

Sam reached into his desk and pulled out a small plastic bag and tossed it on the desk in front of us. "A toy. Her husband had no idea if it had any significance."

Alec picked up the bag and looked at the small orange fuzzy creature.

"That's Greggo," I said, recognizing the character from the *Jackie and Me* children's show.

"Greggo?" Alec asked, looking at me.

"He's a character from the *Jackie and Me* show. Kids love that show. It's a little young for second graders, but maybe she had some of the toys in her classroom."

"What's the premise of the show?" Alec asked.

"I guess you could say it's a do good unto others and have confidence in yourself sort of thing. Greggo has confidence issues, and he spent most episodes learning it's okay to make mistakes. There are about five or six regular characters, and they each have what you might call a weakness, and they interact with one another trying to resolve problems. The character Jackie was sort of the leader. It was really big when Thad and Jennifer were little."

Alec looked at the small toy in his hands. "It does sound a little young for second graders," he said. Then he looked at Sam. "Any other developments?"

"I've told you all I know. We're still searching for answers," he said.

"Okay, well, if you find anything else out, let me know," Alec said.

Alec started to get up when Sam stopped him.

"Have you found out anything on your end?"

"I've interviewed Richard Rose, Hilda Bixby, Janice Cross, and a Josh Stine. I believe I left you a voicemail detailing that. Any of the four could be possible murderers, but none of them are strong suspects. Like you, we're still working on it."

Sam nodded his head. "Okay. Well, let me know if you find out anything."

We said our goodbyes and headed to the car.

"Alec, I may have forgotten to tell you something," I said when we got into the car and had closed the doors.

He sighed loudly and then looked at me. "Why does that not surprise me?"

"Don't take that tone with me," I said.

"What didn't you tell me?" he asked.

"Ask it in a sweet voice," I said.

He sighed again. "Sugar pie, what did lil' ole you forget to tell me?" he asked in a falsetto voice with a bad southern accent.

I grinned. "You stink at Southern accents. And what I forgot to tell you is that Lucy and I did some more investigating."

"And why doesn't that surprise me, either?" he asked.

"Josh Stine's mother is an acquaintance of Lucy's, and we dropped in on her at Walmart, which is where she works. It seems Josh lied about his mother being sick. He actually flunked out of college. She said he was the sensitive type and has some social issues."

"Ah. That doesn't surprise me much, either. He did seem a little awkward. Did she catch on that you were questioning her about him?" he asked.

I snorted. "Please! Lucy and I are not amateur sleuths. We know what we're doing. Now, what do you think about those rings? And the fact that she was tightly gripping that toy?"

He shrugged. "It's still too early to say."

"Do you think they dusted the rings for prints?" I asked.

"I'm sure they did, but I don't know that they could find anything on them. There's not enough surface area for a complete print to be put on them."

"That's true," I agreed. "I think we need to go talk to everyone all over again."

He started the car. "I don't know about that."

"I like having a chauffeur. You could just not buy your own car and keep driving me around."

"Sure," he said and drove off.

Chapter Sixteen

"MOM, I NEED TO DO MY laundry," Jennifer said. She skated across the hardwood floor in her sock feet and stopped in front of me.

"Okay. What's stopping you?" I asked, pinning my wet hair up in a bun. I had just gotten out of the shower and had worked in a leave-in oil treatment, and I wanted to let it soak in without getting all over my clothes.

"You have clothes in the washer. They stink. They've been in there a while, from the smell of it," she informed me.

I sighed. "I forgot. I have to rewash them," I said, heading to the laundry room.

"Oh, Mom," she whined. "I don't have all day."

"It's Saturday, so in fact, you do have all day. I really think it's time you got a part-time job and contributed to your upkeep at school," I said.

The scent of mildew emanated from the washer when I lifted the lid. She wasn't kidding about them stinking. I tried to remember how long it had been since I washed them and thought it might be more than a week. Yikes.

I turned the water to hot and put in extra detergent and set it for a double rinse. I hoped I wouldn't have to toss any of the clothes, but I thought it likely.

"I know what I can do to earn money," Jennifer said from six inches behind my left ear.

I screamed. "Jennifer, I didn't even hear you come in here."

"Yeah, I'm a ninja. Anyway, why don't you pay me for cleaning your house and doing your laundry? This place is practically a pigsty, and you need help," she said.

"Excuse me? This place is not a pigsty!" I insisted. "Sure, I forgot the laundry, and the dishes need washing, but it's not a pigsty."

"And what about the half-inch thick layer of dust on everything?" she asked.

I moved past her and into the kitchen. "That is not a half-inch thick layer of dust. That's a protective coating. There's no way the furniture will get scratched as long as it's there."

I opened the dishwasher and started taking the clean dishes out. I couldn't remember when I had last run the dishwasher, and I had a sink full of dirty dishes. My cat Dixie rubbed up against my leg.

"Hey, boy," I said and bent over and scratched his head. Dixie purred appreciatively and rubbed against my leg.

"Mom, I can come once a week and clean, and you can pay me. Then you won't have to worry about it at all. Besides, don't you have to pass some sort of inspection to be able to cook food for the public? I don't think you'll pass," she said, crossing her arms over her chest.

I stopped, three clean mixing bowls in my hands, and looked at her. "Inspection?"

"Yeah," she said, nodding her head. There was just a touch of sarcasm in her voice. "You need a license or permit or something. The city needs to know you have a clean kitchen that you're cooking in. Otherwise, you'll poison your customers, and Alec will have to investigate you."

"Oh," I said and went to the cupboard I kept the mixing bowls in. I opened the door and slid them in. "What happens if they figure out I don't have one?" I asked.

She sighed loudly. "You are going to get into so much trouble. Probably a fine or something. I don't know all the details, but really, it should be common knowledge."

"All right. I'll pay you to come every week and clean, and I'll look into getting a permit or license or whatever. And we won't tell anyone that I didn't know."

It wasn't that the house was dirty so much as I had just gotten a little behind on the cleaning. And she was right that I should have known about the license. I had gotten caught up in Iris's murder and had forgotten that little detail.

She smirked. "That might cost you a little more."

"I bet it won't," I told her. "You'll keep your mouth closed or you'll be paying your entire college bill."

"Yeah, yeah," she said and poured herself a cup of coffee.

"Hey, Jennifer, do you remember a Josh Stine from school?" I asked as I unloaded the silverware basket into the drawer.

"Yeah. Nerdy. Kind of weird. He was a year ahead of me in school. Why?"

"Weird how?" I asked.

She shrugged. "I don't know exactly. He just seemed kind of intense when he talked to you. He was just a weird kid, I guess. Why?"

"I don't know. He was at Iris Rose's classroom when Alec and I went there. He had her when he was in second grade. Wait," I said, turning toward her. "How could he be a year ahead of you if he was in Iris's class? You had her the first year she taught."

Jennifer stared at me for a second, then jumped up and ran from the kitchen. I followed her into her room where she was sitting on the floor, digging through the bottom drawer of her nightstand.

"What are you looking for?" I asked her.

"Um," she said and kept digging. Finally, she pulled out a school pictures envelope. "I have all the classroom pictures in here. I kept the ones that had all the kids in my class in this one envelope."

She thumbed through the stack and pulled one out. "Here it is. And look, he was in my class in second grade."

She handed the picture to me, and I scanned the faces. He was five faces down from Jennifer, smiling for all he was worth, wearing thick, black-rimmed glasses that were sliding down his nose. His hair was smashed against the side of his head in what was a dead giveaway for a mattress-head hairdo.

"Are you sure he graduated a year before you?" I asked.

She nodded. "Now that I think about it, I think when he was in fifth grade, he skipped to sixth. He was always smart."

"That's odd," I said, sitting down on her bed. "His mother said he flunked out of college. She mentioned that he had some emotional problems and was going to get some therapy, but I would think a really smart kid would still excel in academics."

"College is hard, Mom. You don't know. It's different from when you went," she insisted.

This was coming from my overly sensitive child. Although not a social misfit by any stretch of the imagination, she had found school harder than her outgoing older brother. "Okay, I get it. I really do."

"Do you think he killed Mrs. Rose?" she asked me soberly.

"I don't know. Being odd doesn't make someone a murderer. Tell me, knowing what you know about him and how he was in school, do you think he would be capable of murder?"

She shook her head without hesitation. "No. I really don't. Now Billy Green—I would totally suspect him. He hasn't been around, has he? That kid was creepy weird."

"I do not know a Billy Green, so no, not that I'm aware of," I said and got up. I handed her back the picture. "Do you remember *Jackie and Me*?"

She turned to me. "I haven't thought of that show in years! I loved that show!" She started humming the theme song. "I wish I could remember the words. I need to look up an episode on YouTube for old times' sake."

"Did Mrs. Rose have those characters in her classroom? I thought by the second grade you had outgrown that show," I said.

She thought about it for a minute. "I don't remember. I think I'm getting old."

"Well, if you're old, I'm ancient," I said and stood up and headed back into the kitchen. My laptop was on the kitchen table, and I opened it up.

Jennifer followed me back into the kitchen. "What are you doing?" she asked. "You've got dishes to do."

"I'm looking up requirements to get a license to bake and sell things from my kitchen. And you, my sweet, sweet daughter, have dishes to do. You volunteered, remember?" I said, opening Google.

"I didn't volunteer. You're putting words into my mouth," she protested.

"Get to work or no money. Now," I said, giving her the evil eye.

She sighed. "So much for a weekend off. How much are you going to pay me?"

"I'm keeping that a secret for now." I was inwardly crossing my fingers, hoping the city requirements wouldn't be too harsh.

"You need to print up business cards and flyers and get your new blog up. I don't know why you're wasting so much time," she complained, as she finished emptying the dishwasher.

"Yes, I know. I swear, I am going to do it," I said. "Oh! Good news! I'm going to be known as a cottage food seller."

"Yay," Jennifer replied unenthusiastically. "You should bake some rustic bread. I love bread, and the restaurant sets a bread basket on the table, no matter what you're going to order."

I gasped. "You are so smart. I might ask Cynthia about that."

"I know," she said.

I wasn't sure where she got her smart mouth from. It couldn't have been from me.

Chapter Seventeen

"I NEED SUGAR, BUTTER, flour, cream cheese, and anything else associated with baking ingredients," I said, looking over my list. Alec and I were at Shaw's Market, and I was stocking up. I had gone through my kitchen cupboards and tossed out anything that I didn't absolutely need to make room for more baking supplies.

"It seems to me that you have more than enough baking supplies at your house," Alec pointed out. I had given him the task of pushing the buggy so my hands would be free to fill said buggy.

"No. You can never have enough baking supplies. You should know this by now," I reminded him and picked up a ten-pound sack of sugar. I contemplated getting a second one, but I wasn't sure I'd have room to store it, even with the extra room I had made.

Alec snickered. "You would think I'd know this by now, wouldn't you? You're a bake-a-holic."

"I prefer to call myself the baking queen of Sandy Harbor, thank you very much. Oh, and I have an inspection tomorrow. I can't believe they arranged to do it so quickly, but the inspector is the cousin of one of Lucy's friends, and Lucy pulled some strings for me," I told him.

"Wow, that was fast," he said. "Do you think you'll pass?"

I turned and gave him the evil eye. "Of course I'm going to pass. I've had Jennifer in there scrubbing my kitchen down like she was Cinderella herself. You can eat off my kitchen floors right now."

"Poor Jennifer," he murmured.

"Do you think there's a chance I won't pass?" I asked him, suddenly terrified I wouldn't. How humiliating would it be to have to tell Cynthia that I couldn't bring desserts down to the restaurant because I couldn't pass the health inspection?

"I'm sure you'll do fine. Other than a few dirty dishes in the sink, your kitchen is always spotless," he said.

"Yeah. I've been leaving dirty dishes lately. What's up with that? It's so unlike me. Well, now I've got Jennifer to serve me so I can leave all the dirty dishes I want on the weekends."

"You're nuts," he said and looked over my shoulder. I turned to see what he was looking at, and Richard Rose was standing at the far end of the aisle we were in, looking over the cooking oils.

He looked up and saw us and headed in our direction. "Alec, Allie," he said, nodding at us when he got to us. "I haven't heard much on the investigation. Do either of you know what's going on?"

"It's still in preliminary investigation mode," Alec said. "I'm sure someone will be contacting you soon either for more information, or to keep you up to date."

"Oh. Okay," Richard said, nodding. "You know, Hilda's getting out of control. She waits for me to get home from work, standing out on the landing of her apartment. She screams at me. Calls me a murderer. The whole neighborhood can hear her."

"Wow," I said.

"That could be a problem," Alec said. "I know things aren't good between the two of you but have you tried talking to her when she isn't quite so charged up?"

Richard chuckled. "That would be never. She's nuts. I couldn't take it anymore, so I went to a lawyer and started the process to evict her."

"Oh?" Alec said. "Are you sure you want to do that so soon after Iris's death? She's grieving. Things might settle down eventually."

"I don't have a choice. She's making my life miserable. If she would just shut up and stay in her apartment, I wouldn't even consider doing it. But I can't live like this," he said. His jaw tightened. "I did not murder my wife. I loved my wife. I may have made some mistakes, but I loved her." I could see his eyes getting moist as he spoke.

"Richard, we know that. Death is a horrible thing that adds a lot more tension to situations that are already difficult," I said. I glanced at Alec. The fighting between those two might make either of them snap, and we'd have another murder on our hands.

"You need to remember that she might not be stable right now due to the stress of losing her daughter and try to keep your distance," Alec advised. "Don't let your emotions get the best of you. You don't want to do anything you might regret."

"You really don't want to do that," I agreed.

"You don't know what this is like," he said, clenching his hands into fists at his side. "I lost my wife! I just want to mourn her in peace."

"If you'd like, I'll talk with her. Maybe I can get her to settle down and leave you alone," Alec offered.

"That's a great idea," I said. "I think she'll listen to you, Alec."

"I'd appreciate it," Richard said. "But I still want her out. The sooner she's out of my life, the better. She was nothing but a curse for our entire marriage. I never should have let her move into that apartment, but Iris insisted. She felt sorry for her, even after all she had done to her as a child. That's what I loved about Iris, her sense of empathy for others. But it also caused us a lot of trouble when she couldn't say no."

"Understood," Alec said. "But would you consider allowing her to stay longer so she can find a place to live? If she promises to leave you alone?"

Richard sighed and ran a hand through his hair. "I really don't want that. Maybe I'd consider it if she promised to be out by a set date. But if she says one cross word to me, it's over, and I'm having her evicted."

"I'll see what I can do," Alec said.

"Do you think she's been drinking?" I asked him.

"I think so. I haven't gotten close enough to smell her, but her words are slurred sometimes. It wouldn't surprise me a bit if she was."

"I'll see if I can get her to agree to leave you alone," Alec assured him.

"I'd appreciate that," he said.

"I do have a question for you, Richard," Alec said. "When we brought Iris's things from her classroom to you, there was a journal she kept that detailed her day-to-day activities in the classroom. It had comments about students and her thoughts on them and their behavior and other things that happened in her classroom. Did she keep one every year?"

He nodded. "She did. She loved doing that. She said it helped her to gain insight into the children and their personalities, as well as helped her remember the highlights of her year."

"Would you allow me to read the journal from her first year?" Alec asked. "I'd like to have a look at that one."

I studied Alec. What did he have in mind?

"Her first year? Why?" he asked, puzzled.

"Just call it an investigator's curiosity," Alec said.

"Sure. You can have it as long as I get it back. I've been reading over the one from this year," he said, and his eyes teared up again. "I'll have to look for it, but as long as I get it back, it's no problem."

"Great. I'll stop by tomorrow and have a talk with Hilda," Alec said.

"Okay. I think I know exactly where the older journals are. I'll have it for you."

We said our goodbyes, and we watched him turn the corner of the aisle we were in.

When he was out of sight, I turned to Alec. "You want to see what she had to say about Josh?"

"I do. Also, I'm wondering what she might have had to say about a certain nosy parent of a little red-headed girl named Jennifer. I bet she has a lot to say about her," he said with a grin.

I gasped. "I bet she said I was a darling mother. What else would there be to say?"

"That you were nosey and bossy," he said.

I gasped again. The nerve!

"Oh, look. They have brown sugar. You need some of that, don't you?" he asked, turning away so I couldn't see him smiling.

"I most certainly do. And vanilla, lots of vanilla. But I am not nosey," I said. "That's a vicious rumor started by someone who doesn't know what they're talking about."

"Will you make me a pear tart? I like pear tarts."

"I'll make you something all right," I muttered. "Hey, when do you test for your PI license?"

"In a couple of days," he said and pushed the buggy down the aisle.

"I want to take a test to be your assistant," I said. "I can get a license for that, can't I?"

"No, you just get to bake. That's your job now. And write a blog. That's it," he said as we headed for the produce department.

I sighed. "That's so unfair. I think we need to go out on a real date, and soon. It feels like it's been forever since we've done that."

"A date?" he asked. "What's that?"

"I want to wear a dress and heels, and I want to wear my pearls."

"We went to a funeral. You wore a dress and heels. Isn't that a date?" he asked innocently.

I gave him a sideways look. "That is not a date, smarty pants."

"Well, I think a date can be arranged," he said and put one arm around my waist as we walked down the aisle.

"You're cute. Did you know that?" I asked him.

"Indeed. I did," he said. "Don't forget pears."

Pears. I would not forget the pears. Anything for my Sweet Baboo.

Chapter Eighteen

"YOU'RE GOING TO LET me do the talking, right?" Alec asked as we started up the stairs to Hilda's apartment. He was in front, and I was in the back. I needed to rethink my strategy. If he slipped and fell back, I was a goner. I needed to be in front so that if I slipped on these steep steps, the chances he'd be able to catch me were pretty good.

The door swung open before Alec reached the landing.

"Good morning, Hilda," Alec said.

Hilda stood still, staring at Alec.

"Good morning, Hilda," I called over Alec's shoulder.

Alec stepped onto the landing, and I followed close behind.

"Hilda, may we have a moment of your time?" Alec asked her.

I smiled for all I was worth, hoping it would help ease things. The look on Hilda's face said things were not going well for her. Of course, I already knew this, but I had hoped she would be in a better frame of mind this morning.

"I suppose," she said to Alec, then looked over the railing. I wondered if she thought Richard was nearby listening in.

"Thank you," Alec said, and we followed Hilda into her apartment.

She swung the door closed behind us, and I stopped and stared. The apartment was in stark contrast to how it had looked the two earlier visits I had paid her. There were dirty clothes strewn about the living room floor, and it looked like dishes hadn't been done in days. A plate of dried, half-eaten spaghetti sat on the coffee table, and an empty bottle of whiskey sat on an end table.

I caught Alec looking at the mess sideways, but he didn't miss a beat. "I'm sorry to disturb you Hilda, but it's come to my attention that there may be issues between yourself and Richard. I don't want to stick my nose in where it doesn't belong, but I'd also like for things to remain civil between the two of you. We don't want any trouble."

I stood next to Alec, and I could see Hilda's face turn red.

"What Alec is saying is we both understand that after a death in the family, tensions can run high," I explained quickly.

"He's trying to evict me!" she exclaimed. "An old woman with no place to go! He'd throw me out on the street in a heartbeat! Just like that!" She snapped her fingers for emphasis.

"Hilda, I spoke with Richard. He said you were screaming at him from your apartment. You have to know that's not going to win you any favors with him, right?" Alec asked.

Boy, talk about good cop, bad cop. I wanted to be the bad cop, but I didn't have the heart to do it to someone that had just lost their only child. Apparently, Alec had no problem with it.

"He killed my daughter!" she shouted.

"We are still investigating this murder. No one has been charged yet," Alec pointed out. I don't know where he got his calm from. He seemed to be able to pull it out of his pocket whenever he needed it.

"If you were doing your job, you would have arrested him by now," she said, sounding a little steadier.

Uh oh. Hilda didn't want to play the incompetent cop card. Alec wasn't going to put up with that.

The muscle in Alec's jaw twitched. "Listen, Hilda, we are doing all we can to solve this case. We appreciate your patience."

Hilda closed the short distance between herself and Alec and peered up into his face. "I have no patience when my baby is dead, and the killer lives just a few feet away, fancy-free, doing whatever he feels like," she said.

"Did it ever occur to you that he lost someone he loved, too?" Alec said, not backing down.

Hilda gasped and took a step back. "If he loved her so much, then why is he running around with Janice Cross? They're together, just as I predicted," she said. Her voice cracked, and her eyes filled with tears.

The muscle in Alec's jaw went slack. "I'm sorry. I hadn't heard anything about that. But even if it's true, it doesn't mean he killed your daughter. It just means he doesn't have much in the way of morals, and that's not a crime."

I stood there, shifting from one foot to the other during this exchange, wishing I could be somewhere else. Confrontation was never my strong suit. I'd do it if I felt I had to, but I hated it.

"No. Not having morals isn't a crime. If it was, I suspect most of us would be in jail by now," she whispered.

"Richard is prepared to allow you to stay for a while longer, giving you time to find a place to live, on the condition that you stop behaving the way you have been. No more screaming at him. No contact at all would be best," Alec said softly.

"How long can I stay?" she asked.

"He didn't give me an exact time frame, but we'll pin him down on it. But one slip up, and he'll evict you."

She nodded. "Fine then. I'll start looking. I don't want to have to look at him for the rest of my life anyway," she said.

I felt so bad for Hilda. Life hadn't treated her well, and now it had stolen her only child. I wanted to offer to help her clean the place up, but I knew Alec would frown on that. She needed to get her act together, and she needed to take responsibility for herself.

"We'll be in touch," Alec said and turned for the door. I followed him, and I almost had to run to keep up as he took the steep stairs two at a time.

We walked around the side of Richard's house and headed for his front door.

Richard was at the door before we could knock. He and Hilda must spend a lot of time at the window.

"Good morning, Richard," Alec said, sounding business-like.

"Good morning, come in," he said and held the door open for us. We followed him to the living room and took a seat across from him. I wanted Alec to let him have it over him seeing Janice Cross again, but I didn't know whose side Alec was on right at that moment.

"So, did you talk to her?" Richard asked with a smile.

I wanted to knock that smug look off his face.

"I did. I told her if she agreed not to harass you, you would let her stay until she could find a new place to live, for a limited time, of course. You need to decide on that time frame so I can relay that to her," Alec said. His mood was somber, and so was mine. No one had a right to destroy someone, especially someone that was grieving.

"Great, I appreciate the help. It'll save me some money if I don't have to evict her," Richard said.

"She said you were seeing Janice Cross," Alec said, pausing to see what Richard's reaction would be.

He didn't have to wait long as the smile slid right off of Richard's face. "I am not seeing her. That's long over."

"It's your business if you are," Alec said. "But maybe you should keep it to yourself for the time being."

"I can't believe she told you that! I merely gave Janice a ride home when her car wouldn't start the other day. I happened to stop by the elementary school to speak to the principal. That's all it was," he said.

I didn't believe him. There was something about him that said he was lying.

"Like I said, it's your business. The investigation into your wife's death is ongoing," Alec reminded him.

Richard sighed tiredly and pulled himself together. "I appreciate that. I want to see her murderer put behind bars as soon as possible."

"Did you find the journal?" I asked. I had sat quietly for too long and the tension between Alec and Hilda, and now Alec and Richard, was getting to me. I just wanted to go home and bake something.

"I did," he said and got up and picked up a book off the fireplace mantel. He walked back over and handed it to me.

The book had bright sunflowers on the cover, and when I opened it up, Iris's neat handwriting filled the pages. I swallowed back the lump in my throat. This book was from a time when Iris had been young and hopeful of all the possibilities that life and a new teaching career possessed.

"Thank you," I said.

"We appreciate your cooperation," Alec said, and we got to our feet. "We'll be in touch."

We headed out the door and got into my car with Alec driving. I flipped through the pages, wondering if this book held any clues to her murder, but also knowing it would mention Jennifer from time to time. My heart sometimes ached with the fact that my children were grown. If only I could recapture just a day or two of their young lives. I blinked back the tears.

This journal held a chance for me to relive a part of my daughter's early years.

Chapter Nineteen

"TA-DA!" I SAID, PUSHING a bowl of snow cream in front of Alec.

He looked up from the book he was studying. "What's this?"

"Snow cream. It snowed last night, and I caught some of it. Guaranteed pest, critter, and uh, dead body free snow," I said proudly.

He looked at me. "It's not the same."

"It is the same. I used snow, cream, sugar, and vanilla extract. Trust me. It's the same. Oh, and I have some chocolate syrup to pour over it. I might even have some maraschino cherries in the fridge." I gave him a big smile.

"Wild-caught snow is better," he said.

The smile left my face. "Are you serious?"

"Yeah," he said.

"Alec Blanchard, if you don't at least taste this snow cream that I slaved over a hot stove to make, you are in big trouble," I said.

"A hot stove?"

"Whatever. A cold bowl. Taste it."

"Okay, fine," he said and picked up the spoon in the bowl. He scooped up a small bite-sized amount and tasted it. He smiled. "I guess it is pretty good."

"Told ya so," I said, and went and scooped a bowl for myself. "It's pretty good if I do say so myself."

"Mmm," he said, taking a bigger bite.

"I want to go to Kohl's," I said.

"Why, pray tell?" he asked.

"I might need some baking stuff," I said. I poured chocolate syrup over my snow cream.

He sighed. "It seems like you have more than enough baking stuff."

"I might need more mixing bowls. Or something."

"Fine, we'll go. But one of these days I want to make snow cream with wild-caught snow."

WHEN WE PULLED UP AT Kohl's, I spotted Josh walking across the parking lot. "Hey, Alec," I said and pointed Josh out.

Alec nodded at me. "Let's go before he gets in his car."

We hurried across the parking lot and managed to get in position to be passing him as he headed toward the far side of the parking lot.

"Oh hi, Josh," I called out when we got close.

He stopped in his tracks and stared at us. I wondered if he had forgotten who we were.

He forced himself to smile at us. "Hi," he said quietly.

"How are you doing, Josh?" I asked. He held a small shopping bag in his hand, and his face looked more broken out than it had before.

"I'm-I'm okay," he said, looking away.

"Hi, Josh," Alec said. "I've been meaning to check on you. Just to see how you're doing."

Josh's face turned red. "I'm fine."

"Josh, we know how important Mrs. Rose was to you, and we wanted you to know if there's anything you need, you should feel free to ask," I said gently.

He looked at me, making eye contact. "Thanks. That's nice. It's still hard to believe she's gone."

"Losing someone important to you is hard," Alec said.

"Sometimes I think Mrs. Rose is the only person that made me feel like I could make something of myself." He smiled a little when he said it. "She was always saying, 'you can do it.'"

That made me feel bad. It was hard for shy kids to feel confident, but at least he had had Iris.

"I've heard nothing but good things about Mrs. Rose as a teacher," Alec said.

"Have you found out who killed her yet?" Josh asked, looking at Alec. He was shifting from one foot to the other and seemed to have difficulty making and holding eye contact.

Alec shook his head. "No, not yet. We're hoping to have a break in the case soon. Have you heard anything around town?"

"What? What do you mean?" Josh asked, shifting a little faster now.

Alec shrugged. "Sometimes in small towns, things get said. I just wondered if you'd heard anyone say anything about the case."

"Oh," he said, nodding his head. "No, I haven't heard a thing. I've been home taking care of my mother. I have to go now, she's expecting me."

"Okay, well, you let us know if you hear anything," Alec said as Josh hurried off.

I looked at Alec. "He has to take care of his mom?"

"And he sure seemed nervous," he said.

"That he did," I said, and we headed to the store entrance.

"I wonder what he would have done if we had told him we knew his mother wasn't sick?" Alec asked me.

"Probably cry. I think if he knew that we knew he had flunked out of college, he would fall apart," I said.

"If he had, you would have had to take care of him. I handled the funeral scene," he said with a chuckle.

"I think all of our suspects are due for another round of questioning," I told him.

"That could be. And hopefully, Sam has more information from his side of the investigation."

Chapter Twenty

"GIVE ME A KISS BEFORE you go," I said, leaning in toward Alec.

He kissed me and pulled me to him. "I'm only going to be gone a few hours," he assured me.

I giggled. "I know, I know. I just wish you were going to be here when the inspector comes."

"You'll be fine. You and Jennifer have been scrubbing and cleaning for days. That kitchen is shining. The whole house is spotless. No way will you not pass," he assured me.

"Yeah, I guess you're right," I said. "I shouldn't worry."

He let me go. "And if you don't pass, we'll just make whatever changes need to be made and there'll be another inspection. Easy as can be."

"You're right. We can do that."

"All right. I'm leaving now so I won't be late," he said and headed to my car parked out front.

"Good luck!" I called.

He waved at me and got into the car. I watched until he drove out of sight. I knew he didn't need luck. He knew all he needed to know about the law and getting his PI license.

I went back into the house and took another look at the kitchen. Alec was right. It was sparkling clean. I went back into the living room and picked up Iris's journal, and sat on the sofa.

I turned to the first page and read the entry.

August 19

I cannot wait to start the school year. Next week I have to report to the school for meetings. Then I get my classroom and can decorate it! I've wanted to decorate my own classroom for forever, and I can't wait to meet my kids. My kids. I love the sound of that.

Iris was so young and sweet, it broke my heart. So full of hope and potential.

September 3

I made it through my first day. I was so nervous! The kids are so cute and I can't wait to get to know each one.

She had made a list of each child's name and a comment with her first impressions. I skipped down to Jennifer's name.

Jennifer McSwain — Sweet little girl. She has pretty strawberry blond hair and a bright smile. I'm looking forward to teaching her.

My heart swelled with pride. Jennifer had been one of the sweetest little girls. I sometimes felt sorry for other mothers because they didn't have her. I skipped down to Josh Stine's name.

Joshua Stine — quiet, shy boy. He seems a little immature compared to the other children, but very bright.

I started skimming the journal, looking for pages mentioning either Jennifer or Josh. There was an entry where Jennifer had been a big help with passing out art supplies. Another where she had been kind and shared her lunch with a child that had forgotten hers at home. That was my little Jennifer. Always a helper. I decided I was going to make copies of the pages that mentioned Jennifer. She would love to have a copy of them, and I wanted a copy for myself.

I found an entry about Josh where she went into more detail about his personality.

I'm a little concerned about Josh Stine, but I don't know if I should bring it up with someone or not. He seems very immature compared to the other students. He has trouble socializing with the other children, and he frequently has outbursts. On the other hand, he's very smart. He catches on to everything much faster than the other children, but this seems to ostracize him from the others. I am trying to encourage him to help me teach the other children with their math. This makes him very happy. But it doesn't take much for him to become angry. He frequently has tantrums. I just don't know if I should mention all this to someone or not. What if it's nothing and I'm blowing this out of proportion? I can't wait for the day when I'm experienced enough to know how to handle these types of things.

I smiled. Poor Iris. I could imagine it was difficult to know how to handle kids with problems at the beginning of her teaching career.

And then on the last day of school:

Today was harder than I expected. I will miss my kids. They are all so wonderful in their own way. If I had a favorite, it would have to be Jennifer McSwain, although I would never tell anyone that. I've met her father several times, and I'm sure she must take after him. He seems so kind and helpful. I'll miss Jennifer the most, I think. We both cried when she had to leave.

My chest just about burst with pride. That was my girl. So sweet. *Hey, wait a minute.* Why did she assume Jennifer took after Thaddeus? Iris had spent more time around me than she had Thaddeus. I had volunteered to help at the Valentine's Day party and the Christmas party and just about anything else that had come up. Oh well. Jennifer would enjoy reading what Iris had to say about her.

Then I read the entry about Josh:

I'm concerned about Joshua Stine. He's been struggling this last week with the knowledge that he wouldn't be in my class anymore. He was inconsolable this last day. Although I enjoyed having him in my class, he was exhausting at times. I requested that he get some help before he goes into third grade. His mother was not receptive. She insists he doesn't have any issues, but I spoke with the school psychologist, and she agreed with me. We could not get his mother to agree to counseling.

Hmm. Iris didn't go into detail about exactly what her concerns were regarding Josh, but his mother had been made aware. When Lucy and I spoke to her several days earlier, she had suggested her son needed some therapy, so obviously, she was no longer in denial. He had been an overly emotional child, and it looked like not much had changed. I would have to go back over the journal more carefully to see if I had missed what Iris thought the root of the problem was.

The doorbell rang, and I put the journal down and went to answer it.

"Good morning, Allie McSwain?" the man standing at the door asked. "I'm Ken Matson. I'm with the health department."

"Yes, please come in," I said and took a step back.

"Thank you," he said, stepping into the living room.

"Follow me, and I'll show you to the kitchen," I said and led the way. "I've never had an inspection like this before. I hope everything's going to be okay."

"It'll be quick," he said. "I just need to take a look around."

"Please, go ahead," I said, and leaned back against the wall. I crossed my fingers as he went about his job.

He opened cupboards and looked into the stove. I half expected him to be wearing a pair of white cotton gloves and for him to swipe his index finger across the stovetop. Instead, he just looked at everything.

"Is this the refrigerator you're going to use?" he asked.

I nodded. "Yes, that's it."

"You might want to consider getting a second one that's just for the food you're cooking that's for sale. It makes it easier to keep things separate and also for inspections. You don't have to, but you might consider it," he said and took a thermometer out of his briefcase and stuck it into the refrigerator and closed the door. "We need to make sure it's the correct temperature."

"Oh, I hadn't even thought of that," I said.

"Will you be selling hot food?" he asked.

"Not really," I said. "I mean, apple pie's better when it's a bit warm, but I don't need to serve it warm."

"Okay, sounds good. If you were going to sell it hot, there are heat temperature requirements," he said, filling out a form. After a few minutes, he reached back into the refrigerator and looked at the thermometer and then put it back in his briefcase.

"Is it okay?" I asked.

"Perfect. Here you go," he said, handing me a copy of the form he was filling out.

"Good luck on your new business venture, Mrs. McSwain," he said and headed for the front door.

"What? That's it?" I said, following him. "I passed?"

"With flying colors," he said over his shoulder. "Consider that second refrigerator, and don't forget you are subject to inspection at any time."

"Oh, thank you!" I said, and he was gone. I had done it. I had passed the inspection, and I was ready to start my business. I could hardly believe it.

I grabbed my phone off the coffee table and texted Alec.

I did it! I passed! Yippee!!

He was probably still taking the PI test, or maybe he was driving home now, so I would have to wait to talk to him. I sat back on the sofa and smiled to myself. This was going to be awesome. I was sure of it.

Chapter Twenty-One

ALEC WAS TRUE TO HIS word and took me out to a fancy restaurant. Fancy for Sandy Harbor, anyway. I had bought a new black dress at a local dress shop just for this occasion. I'd also worn my simple strand of pearls. Sandy Harbor needed more dress-up restaurants, so I could feel like a girly girl more often.

We went to Le Chemise, a new French restaurant that had recently opened in town. The place was packed, and the décor had old-world charm. Two white candles and a bunch of fresh grapes and woven grapevine made up the table centerpiece. The display sat on a gold charger was heavy and rustic looking and reminded me of something that would have been made in the eighteenth century. Whoever had opened this restaurant knew what they were doing with the décor.

I was eyeing their dessert menu and was impressed with their offerings and wondered who was making them. I couldn't think of anyone in town that baked French-style pastries. I was going to have to investigate this more fully.

"Do you see anything that looks good to you?" Alec asked me.

"I've got my eye on the Lamb Navarin. What about you?" I asked. I hadn't had a nice lamb stew in a long time. Thaddeus and I had vacationed in Normandy before the children were born, and I had fallen in love with the lamb stew we'd had.

"Lamb is always a good choice. I'm thinking of a classic coq au vin. I haven't had that in what seems like years," he said, still looking over the menu. "And how about a nice red wine?"

"Sounds good. I wonder if it's an authentic French wine?" I asked, still eyeing the dessert menu.

"Let's hope so," he said. "And what on that dessert menu has caught your attention? I know something must-have."

I looked up at him. His eyes had never left his own menu, but he knew what had caught my eye. "All of it. I mean, they couldn't possibly be authentic, right?"

He looked at me with a smirk on his lips. "What makes you say that? It's a French restaurant, isn't it? Surely they wouldn't *lie* about the authenticity, would they?" he asked, emphasizing the word lie.

I narrowed my eyes at him. "I don't know anyone in town that can bake authentic French desserts," I whispered.

"I detect a note of jealousy in that statement," he said. "How about a nice Bordeaux?"

"I have nothing to be jealous of," I said. "Order any wine you want. I don't care."

"Now, Allison, let's not get huffy. I'm sure you have nothing to worry about where desserts are concerned. Right?"

"No, I do not have anything to worry about. And don't call me Allison. Only my mother calls me Allison," I huffed. I wasn't worried about competition. Le Chemise was a new restaurant, and it stood to reason it would be packed for the first few weeks it was open. But after the novelty had worn off, it would only do a decent business if the food was really good. I did have to admit, it was poor timing since I was getting ready to begin offering my desserts at Henry's. But I had an advantage this place didn't. I had a reputation for baking the finest desserts in town.

"So are we settled on our meal?" he asked, laying his menu down.

I nodded. "I think so."

"Why don't you order a dessert of your choice, and I'll order one of mine, and that way you'll have two items off their menu that you can try out. You know, and see if they taste authentic or not," he asked.

I narrowed my eyes at him again. "I do not need to try out their desserts. I know no one in town knows how to make French pastries."

He shrugged. "Okay. But I have my eye on that St. Honore'."

I gasped. "Oh, St. Honore' is wonderful. I mean, it's wonderful if it's authentic."

"Well, let's hope it is. And what will you be having?" he asked.

"I'll have the Chocolate Religieuse."

He smiled, and the waiter walked up. He wore an actual suit, and I was impressed. No other restaurant in town had their wait staff dress up like that. The closest we had was Antonio's Italian restaurant and the wait staff there merely wore white dress shirts and black dress pants.

"Good evening, Monsieur, Madame," he said in a thick French accent, nodding at each of us in turn. "May I take your order?"

My mouth nearly dropped open. He was French. That meant the food was most likely authentic. And if the food was authentic, then the desserts were too. I forced myself not to make eye contact with Alec.

When the waiter left, Alec said, "Wow. Authentic."

"Don't start. Just because the waiter is French doesn't mean anything."

"Hey, I'm not going to give you a hard time. I didn't think this place would be authentic-authentic. I just figured someone took a French cooking class," he said.

"Me too," I said, suddenly feeling deflated.

"Hey, don't you get down. You're one of the best bakers around. You have nothing to worry about," he assured me.

"I know. I'm being silly," I said.

"That's right, you are," he said.

The wine came, and Alec poured us each a glass.

"That looks good," I said.

"Let's toast to your new business venture, and me hopefully passing the PI exam," he said passing me a glass and holding his up.

"There's no 'hopefully' about it. I know you passed that exam with flying colors," I said as we gently brought our glasses together.

"This is going to be a great year," he said and took a sip from his glass. "Allie?"

I looked at him. His eyes were shiny.

"I love you. I mean, really, really love you."

"Oh, Alec, I love you too," I said and felt tears spring to my eyes. "And now you're going to make me cry and my mascara is going to run all over the place."

"I like it that way. It will give you that Alice Cooper look I love so much," he said.

I laughed and got up and kissed him, and then sat down again.

"Okay, don't make me cry all over the place and make people look at me," I said and dabbed at my eyes with my napkin.

"I won't if you won't," he said.

Our food was brought in gold bowls similar to the charger in the centerpiece, but they were more modern and practical. It smelled wonderful, and my stomach growled.

"This smells so good," I said.

"Bon appétit," the waiter said and left us alone.

"This looks good, too," Alec said.

I took a bite of my Lamb Navarin, making sure to get a bit of lamb and potato on my spoon, and groaned. "This is so good," I said after I'd swallowed. "I mean, really, really good."

"That's what I was going to say," Alec said.

Le Chemise wasn't going to have any problem drawing a crowd. I didn't think the novelty would ever wear off if they served food this good every night. I was enjoying the food, but I was starting to worry a little for Henry's.

"I hope this place doesn't hurt Henry's business," I said to Alec.

"I doubt it. It's completely different types of food. Besides, the prices reflect the quality of the food, and everyone isn't going to be able to afford this place regularly," he replied.

"That's true," I said. "Did you get a chance to look over Iris's journal?" I was so excited about the restaurant that I almost forgot about the journal.

"Not really. I planned on reading it tonight," he said. "You?"

"I did. And as I expected, Jennifer was her star student. Iris appreciated the shy student. It's refreshing, really. So many teachers complained about her being so quiet, but Iris saw how wonderful she is," I said.

Alec smiled. "And you aren't a bit biased. I think she is, too."

"And then there was Josh Stine," I said, leaning closer to him.

"Oh?" he said, taking a sip of his wine.

I nodded. "She recognized that he had some issues, but didn't say exactly what they were. Just that he was overly emotional and cried for days before the last day of the year. He had issues separating from her, I think."

"Well, he hasn't changed much. He's still overly emotional. Anything else?" he asked.

I shrugged. "I mostly skimmed, looking for Jennifer and Josh's names. I need to re-read it. I want to make copies of the whole thing. I think Jennifer would like to have a copy. I don't think Richard would mind, do you?"

"I doubt it," he said. "He seems reasonable."

The dinner portions were perfect. I normally left food behind at most other restaurants, but not here. It was too tasty to leave anything behind, and the portions weren't too large.

Our dinner plates were removed from the table, and dessert was brought out. They were beautiful to look at. I looked at Alec over my Chocolate Religieuse. Wow, I mouthed at him. It was like a mini tower of pastry, ganache, and whipped cream. He nodded and smiled.

I picked up my fork and dived in. When the ganache hit my mouth, I nearly cried. It was perfectly smooth and creamy. I moved it around in my mouth and looked at Alec wide-eyed. He was staring back at me, equally wide-eyed. I swallowed.

"Oh, Alec, I think I'm in trouble," I whispered.

There was a small mountain of glazed pastries and whipped cream sitting in front of him.

"Stop that. You are not in trouble. This is quite wonderful, to be honest, but so is everything you make. And your recipes are—well, they have that Southern twist, you know?"

"They're plain. That's what you mean, right? My desserts are plain."

"Stop it, Allie. You have a following with your desserts. People love them. Everything will be fine," he said as he forked up more pastry goodness and popped it in his mouth.

I stared at the Chocolate Religieuse in front of me. This might very well be the undoing of me.

Chapter Twenty-Two

I SLEPT FITFULLY THAT night, and I wasn't sure if it was because I was worried about baking my first pie for sale to the public in the morning, or if I suddenly felt like I had competition with the new French restaurant. I tossed and turned, with images floating through my mind, and occasionally dreaming. I dreamt about Iris at one point.

"Allie," she called.

I was sitting on a lawn chair at the lake in Goose Bay, Alabama. I have no idea how she knew how to find me there or why I was even there in the first place.

"Allie," she called again.

I looked up at her. "Iris. How are you?"

She ignored my question, which was probably best. "Allie, you know who did it."

"I do?" I asked. I was puzzled by that statement because at this point, it could have been anyone.

She nodded. She was wearing a pink business casual outfit that consisted of slacks and a blouse with one of those big bows at the neck that was so popular in the early eighties.

"Remember?"

I shook my head.

"You can do it!" she said emphatically.

"Well, I'm trying," I said.

"You can do it!" she said again, just as emphatically as the first time.

I nodded slowly as the sun behind her got brighter. "Okay. I'll try."

"You can do it!" she shouted.

"Oh, okay," I said as the sun blinded me. I put up my hand to shield my eyes from the sun.

"You can do it!" she shrieked and was gone.

I blinked, and the sun disappeared.

The dream was nearly forgotten when my alarm clock went off, and I jumped out of bed. It was 6:00 a.m., and I had just enough time to bake a couple of pies and a cake and get them down to Henry's before the lunchtime crowd came in.

I jumped out of bed and hurried to get dressed. I had so much to do.

I had decided on a dark chocolate cake and the blueberry sour cream pie recipe I had been working on. I thought when we got closer to spring I would try to convert the blueberry sour cream recipe to cherry in honor of cherry blossoms being in bloom.

As I worked, I kept one eye on the clock. I may have set some kind of speed baking record. I put the finishing touches on the chocolate cake, making swirl patterns in the frosting and then shaving dark chocolate to sprinkle around the top. I had bought a pretty crystal cake stand to display the cake on and loaded everything up in my car and headed to Henry's. My stomach did flip-flops on the way over.

I SIGHED WHEN I GOT back home, tossed my purse on the sofa, and sat down for a minute. It was after 1:00. I had been so excited to see if my pies and cakes would sell, I had hung out at Henry's a lot later than I had planned. My feet ached, and I needed a nap.

I decided instead to get on the treadmill. A nap would leave me groggy, and I had skipped my workout the day before. I went to the mudroom and laced up my running shoes, and grabbed a bottle of water from the kitchen. It was better to get it done without thinking about it, or I would change my mind and take that nap and fall further behind in my training.

I put my phone on the shelf on my treadmill and started it up. I plugged my earbuds into the phone and popped them into my ears. *Brown Sugar* was first on my playlist. I stepped onto the deck, starting slowly, letting my mind wander as my body warmed up.

The dream from the night before drifted across my mind. It was nice that Iris had encouraged me, but I was baffled as to who the killer was. Why hadn't she just told me in the dream? And what was I doing at the lake in Goose Bay? I had never enjoyed going to the lake. You never knew what was swimming in that murky water.

I kicked the treadmill up a notch.

You can do it!

I smirked. "Sure I can, Iris."

I needed to get to work on the blog. I was already baking, and I didn't want to let it all go to waste. I wondered if taking pictures on my old digital camera would be good enough or if I should buy a new camera. Probably needed a new camera, I thought.

You can do it!

"Sure, Iris."

I had also been looking at pretty tablecloths online. I wanted to get an assortment as backdrops for my pictures. But as far as that went, I could go to the fabric store and buy a yard or two of different prints and patterns. I turned the treadmill up a couple more notches and felt my breathing deepen.

You can do it!

"Oh, shut up, Iris. I've got planning to do," I muttered.

You can do it! You can do it! You can do it!

My mind went to Iris. I didn't particularly want to dream about her. I hated dreaming. I preferred to be in control of where my mind went, and dreams were out of my control. I turned the treadmill up faster and stretched my legs out. I liked running fast better than long, but the marathon would stretch me both physically and mentally. It was going to take a lot of self-control to keep from giving up before I hit the finish line.

My mind wandered to Iris's journal. It was a real treasure to have her words about Jennifer. Any parent would be proud of their child, and this was just the icing on the cake.

I breathed in deeply and took a swig of water. I can do it. I can do it. I needed to keep this frame of mind during the marathon.

Then it hit me. My stomach dropped, and I lost my footing and slipped off the treadmill, pulling the red plastic key on the lanyard out of the machine and stopping the motor. I hit the treadmill deck, landing on my side. My head hit the side rail on the way down, and I lay there, stunned.

You can do it.

Chapter Twenty-Three

I MUST HAVE PASSED out because when I sat up and looked at my phone that was still attached to me by the earbuds, it was 3:02. I sat for a minute, trying to remember what I was supposed to be doing. Did I have pies to bake? And then I remembered and stumbled to my feet. My head was aching, and I had lost a layer of skin on the underside of my right forearm.

My mouth was dry, and my tongue felt glued to the roof of my mouth. I found my bottle of water lying by the side of the treadmill, and I struggled to get the lid off. When I had managed to unscrew the lid, it slipped out of my fingers and rolled beneath the treadmill deck. I took a deep drink from the bottle and forced myself to my feet. I managed to limp into the kitchen and set the water bottle down. I looked at my phone, trying to remember what I was doing.

I grabbed my keys from the kitchen counter and went into the living room and found my purse. I hobbled out to my car and got in.

MY HEAD WAS POUNDING as I pulled up to the elementary school and parked. There were only three cars left in the teacher's parking lot. I headed to the double front doors and pulled one open. The halls were empty, but I saw lights on in two classrooms. Iris would probably have been working late had she still been alive. I was still wearing my running shoes, and they squeaked on the tile floors. I tried to walk lightly, but it didn't help much. There was no way to sneak up on anyone in this place.

I turned down the hallway leading to Iris's classroom, and that's when I saw him. Josh was sitting on the floor next to Iris's closed door. The room was dark. His head was in his hands, and he didn't look up as I approached him.

"Josh?" I said quietly.

He was rocking slightly but didn't look up.

"Josh?" I said a little louder.

He slowly looked up at me. His face was bright red, and his eyes swollen from crying.

"Hey," I said, trying to sound friendly. My heart pounded in my chest. Now that I was here, I realized I didn't have a plan. "Are you okay?"

He shook his head.

"Do you want to talk about it?" I asked.

He shook his head again.

I wanted to call Alec, but I didn't want to do it in front of him.

"Do you want me to call your mom for you?" I asked. Maybe if she came down here, he would tell her what happened. His emotional state didn't look good, and he might talk to her.

"You know, it's not my fault," he suddenly said.

"What's isn't your fault?" I asked innocently.

"That Mrs. Rose is dead," he said. His voice cracked on the word dead.

"No one thinks it's your fault," I said. "I'm sure of that."

He looked up at me. "That's not true. You and that detective think it's my fault." He said it quietly, but his eyes blazed with anger.

"You shouldn't worry about that. That's just how detectives are. They don't mean anything by it," I said, wishing I had texted Alec before coming to the school.

Before I knew what was happening, Josh had launched himself at me, and I fell backward on the hard floor, hitting my head. The thick knit cap cushioned the blow very little, and I felt things go black again. I woke up a few moments later, and I wondered where Alec was before I realized I was being dragged.

"Wha?" I mumbled, trying to find my words.

My head rolled to the side as we passed a classroom with a light still on. I moaned and tried to call out for help, but all that came out was a mumbled, "Wha?" The door was closed, and no one came.

I heard Josh sobbing and tried to get a look at him. He had hold of both of my legs and pulled me along the waxed floor. I couldn't lift my head high enough off the floor to get a good look at him. I groaned.

If I could find my phone, I could call Alec. Except that I couldn't speak intelligible words for some reason. My tongue felt swollen and foreign in my mouth, and I couldn't remember words. Pain surged through my head, and I groaned again and willed myself to get my wits about me.

After a few minutes, my head began to clear a little, and Josh suddenly stopped dragging me. He sat down beside me. "It wasn't my fault," he breathed near my ear. "I just wanted to talk to her. To tell her how important she was to me. I told her I loved her, but she said she was married and didn't want me. I bought her a ring, but she didn't want it. But it wasn't my fault. None of it was my fault."

He sat back, breathing hard. "She was the only person that told me I was worth anything. She told me I could do it. Whatever it was that I wanted to do, I could do it."

"What about your mother?" I said weakly, finally finding my words. "Didn't she tell you that you could do it?" I slowly reached for my phone in my pocket. I couldn't recall what had happened to my purse.

He laughed bitterly. "No. She said to be careful. She said you're different. You can't do things other kids can do."

"Mothers worry," I squeaked out, still trying to make my way to my jeans pocket without him seeing me.

"She didn't want me to leave her. She didn't want me going to Texas. She was so glad when I flunked out. She was happy about it," he said. "She got what she wanted. But I didn't get what I wanted."

"It's hard for a mother to let her kids go. It's only because they love their kids," I said and felt the bump in my pocket. I gently slipped the phone out and hid it in my hand, keeping it by my side.

"You don't know what love is," he said without emotion. "No one but me and Mrs. Rose knows what love is."

He suddenly turned to me and shoved me. I grabbed for purchase and realized I was at the stairs entrance. I felt myself falling, and I reached up and grabbed the chain that was strung across the entrance, and I held on with all my might as he shoved me again. My phone flew down the stairs, and I found my voice and screamed.

"I didn't want to do it," he said, pushing me again. "Let go!"

I screamed with everything I had, and my head screamed back. I felt vomit rising in my throat and thought I might choke on it, but I kept screaming.

"Hey! What are you doing?" I heard a male voice shout from what seemed far away.

"Let go!" Josh hissed at me and punched me in the side of the head.

Everything went black as I felt myself falling.

Chapter Twenty-Four

I LAY ON THE HOSPITAL bed with Alec sitting at my side. The lights seemed so bright, and my eyes swam with spots. There was a needle in my arm, and a bag of fluids hung on a metal rack beside me. I hoped there were pain meds in there because I needed some. I moaned.

"Hey," Alec whispered, leaning toward me.

"Hey," I said back, my throat cracking.

"How are you feeling?" he asked.

"Horrible," I squeaked out.

He leaned over and pressed his lips to my forehead. "I'm so sorry," he whispered.

"What happened?" I asked, trying to force the memories to come.

"Josh tried to shove you down the stairs at the elementary school. But one of the teachers, Mike Evans, heard you scream, and he stopped him. Unfortunately, Josh had already hit you in the head, and that's why you're here," he said, gently brushing the hair off my forehead. "You also took a tumble about halfway down the stairs."

I tried to smile, but the skin on my face felt tight. "Did he confess?"

"He did. I just spoke with Sam Bailey. Josh said he accidentally knocked Iris down the stairs. It seems he went to see her and confess his love for her."

"He did it," I said, already knowing that fact.

"Josh had been making appearances at the school for a couple of weeks before her death. When Iris rejected him, he got angry and shoved her. He swears he didn't mean to kill her, but he panicked and took her out into the woods and had a burial for her. That was his ring we found on Iris's finger. He tried to give it to her that day. He said she wouldn't take it."

"Poor Iris," I whispered.

"Why did you go to the school?" he asked.

"Greggo," I answered.

Alec's forehead furrowed. "Greggo?"

I nodded, but pain shot through my head. "The little orange toy that was in Iris's hands. In the show, he's full of doubts. But one of the other characters, Jackie, always encouraged him. She kept saying, 'you can do it'. I had a dream, and Iris kept saying, 'you can do it,'" I said and swallowed. My mouth was dry, and my lips were chapped.

"Here," he said and brought a straw to my lips for me to take a sip. The water was room temperature, but it felt like heaven in my hot, dry mouth. I swallowed.

"He said Iris was the only person that believed in him and encouraged him. Remember? When we ran into him at Kohls. He said it again today at the school."

Alec sighed. "Too bad he killed the only person that believed in him."

"Yeah. That's pretty sad."

"But, at least we got a confession," he said.

"Do you think it's true? That he didn't mean to do it?" I asked him.

"It could be. But he had better get a good lawyer. I don't think a jury's going to be willing to believe it was an accident when he tried to do it a second time with you," he said. He leaned over and kissed my forehead.

I teared up. "That was so close," I said.

"I know, baby. It's okay. Everything's okay," he murmured.

I was beginning to think being an assistant PI might be bad for my health. I enjoyed spending time with Alec. Except for the near-death experiences I was having, anyway. I was going to have to think about this assistant PI thing carefully.

Sneak Peek

Love is Murder
A Freshly Baked Cozy Mystery, book 6
Chapter One

It had been two weeks since I began blogging, baking, and selling my wares at Henry's Home Cooking Restaurant. Henry Hoffer's widow, Cynthia Hoffer, and I had an arrangement. I would bake up a storm and sell my goodies on consignment at the restaurant. No risk to her. If my cakes and pies didn't sell, I bore the expense. If they did sell, she got a commission. To say it had been a successful venture was an overstatement. Most days I baked too much and had a lot of leftovers. A couple of times, I had under-baked and left Cynthia's customers wanting what they couldn't have. Neither situation was good, and I needed to come up with a better plan.

It was February, and I was working on cooking up something for Valentine's Day. I knew Henry's would be packed on the big day, and I didn't want to disappoint anyone by coming up short. Everyone knows chocolate and Valentine's Day go hand in hand like peanut butter and jelly, so I was working on something rich and chocolaty.

So far I had narrowed it down to a dark chocolate cake with raspberry filling and a strawberry chocolate truffle cheesecake. I wondered if I should come up with an alternate dessert as well. I didn't want to leave out people with chocolate allergies.

"What are you doing?" Alec asked, looking up from his Kindle. Alec was an avid reader, and I loved that about him. My boyfriend was as smart as he was handsome.

"Trying to figure out what to bake for Valentine's Day," I said, flipping through my grandmama's stained and worn recipe cards. Most of what she had baked came from her memory, but they usually began with a basic recipe of some sort. She made changes along the way, adding a little more of this and leaving a lot of that out. I cherished these age-yellowed cards. As a child, I had spent many a rainy afternoon at her house helping her to bake a warm, cozy sweet to brighten the day.

"Chocolate," he said, turning back to his Kindle. He was stretched out on my sofa, shoes on the floor beside him. His dark hair needed a trim. It was falling over his impossibly blue eyes.

"Ya think?" I asked.

"Ayup," he answered without looking up.

"I wonder if I could convert her decadent chocolate cake to a decadent white chocolate cake?" I mused. "That way people would have a choice. It could come in both flavors. Raspberry filling would be good in either of them."

"You could make one side of the cake white and one chocolate," he suggested.

"Oh, that would be beautiful!" I said, picturing it in my mind. I had some large, fourteen-inch round cake pans that would work. I could set up a divider of some sort when I baked the layers and then remove the divider and put the layers together. But then I realized that the white chocolate would be touching the dark chocolate, and that might be a problem for some with allergies.

I sighed and continued flipping through the cards. Grandmama had kept the recipe cards in an old tin recipe box that had an orange floral design on the box. I picked up a card that had a chocolate chip cookie recipe on it and smiled. I was instantly transported back to my nine-year-old self on a rainy day in March. I had wanted cookies. There was a dark smudge in the corner, and I was the reason for that smudge. The chocolate chips were too tasty to resist, and I had been shoving handfuls of them in my mouth when Grandmama wasn't looking. They had melted in my hand, and when I picked up the card, I left a chocolate smudge in the corner. A tear sprang to my eye, and I brushed it away.

Alec's phone rang, and he reached for it on the coffee table. He glanced at it, then sat up and put his Kindle down. "Alec Blanchard," he said, answering the phone.

"Yes?" he murmured. "I see."

I continued flipping through the recipes, and now and then, glancing over at Alec. He was mostly silent, only making a few noncommittal sounds here and there. He had whipped out his notebook and started jotting something down.

Finally, he said goodbye and hit end on the phone.

I looked at him with a raised eyebrow.

"I've got my first case," he said and smiled at me.

Alec had retired from being a police detective at the end of December and had taken and passed the Maine PI test a couple of weeks ago. I was proud of him for venturing out on his own.

He hadn't gotten along well with the local police chief, and he had become restless.

"Congratulations!" I said excitedly. "So, what's the scoop?"

He narrowed his eyes at me. "Allie, I'm working for myself now. I have to keep people's business confidential or word will get around, and there won't be any repeat business."

"Alec, consider me an employee of yours. Or practically an employee, anyway. I'm going to help you with the investigations. I am completely trustworthy," I said, giving him a military salute.

"And you tend to gossip and tell your gossipy friend everything," he pointed out.

I gasped. "I am not gossipy! And neither is Lucy!"

"Oh?" he asked, cocking one eyebrow at me.

"Alec Blanchard! Lucy and I have been a big help to you on past cases. Admit it. We've gotten you information that you never would have gotten on your own," I reminded him.

He looked up at the ceiling and sighed. "I guess that's true. You both have come up with some important information from time to time," he admitted. "But I don't want to break anyone's trust. This town is too small, and once I get a reputation for not keeping things confidential, there'll be no way to gain back the public's trust."

Now it was my turn to sigh. "Listen, Sherlock Holmes, I completely understand. You want professionalism. I promise I will be completely professional. Scout's honor," I promised, now giving him the Girl Scout salute.

He shook his head slowly. "You are something else. Do you know who Meg Cranston is?" he asked.

I brightened. "No, I don't think I do. But what about her?"

He leaned back against the back of the sofa. "She thinks her husband's cheating. She wants me to get proof."

"A cheating husband? That's it?" I asked, disappointed. I had helped Alec solve several murders over the past few months, and I rather enjoyed it. Except for the times I nearly became a murder victim myself. Hunting killers has its drawbacks.

"Sorry, Watson," he said with a smirk. "Being a PI will probably be pretty boring compared to being a police detective."

"All right. Fine. I'll have to adjust my expectations." I returned my attention to my recipe cards. "What are the husband's and the probable girlfriend's names?"

"Spencer Cranston and Jenna Maples."

I thought for a minute. "Neither of those names sounds familiar. It seems like more and more people are moving to town these days, though. Maybe they're recent transplants."

"Could be," Alec mused. "Oh, and by the way, I've rented an office. The place isn't much to look at, and I'll need to do some renovations. Since you're my self-appointed assistant, I'll expect you to do your share of the work."

"What?" I paused, slowly looking up from my recipe cards.

He nodded. "Ayup," he said, laying his Maine accent on thick. "Needs new carpet and painting. I didn't venture into the bathroom, but by the smell that was coming through the open door, I'm pretty sure it needs a good scrubbing. I'm assigning that job to you."

"No. I don't think so," I said, scrunching up my face. "I don't do bathrooms. And where is it located?"

"Aster Street."

I thought about it, trying to picture where it was. "Wait. There's only one office building on Aster Street that I can think of. Isn't that the same building the mayor's office is in?"

"The one and only. Just think of all the excitement that must go on down there. And we'll get to be a part of it," he said.

I chuckled. "I bet Bob Payne will be thrilled to see us every day."

Bob Payne was a loan officer at the Bank of Maine by day and mayor of Sandy Harbor by night. Alec and I were not high on the mayor's list of favorite people. It wasn't our fault. Killers had to be caught, and just because he was in denial about certain suspects didn't mean we were going to let them go free.

"He'll adjust," Alec asserted. "But I need to get the repairs and painting done. I need an office where I can see clients. It isn't an ideal location, being upstairs, but the rent was cheap, and I didn't have to sign a lease. It will work for now."

"What about if you have clients that can't manage the stairs?" I asked.

"I guess I'll have to figure out another place to meet them," he said. "I think we should start cleaning first thing in the morning."

"Oh, wait, I have cakes to bake," I reminded him. The mayor's office hadn't been updated since 1976, and I was certain a lot of work would be involved with this little cleanup.

"I'll help you with your baking, and you can help me with my cleaning. How does that sound?" he asked.

I smiled at him. "That sounds like fun, Sherlock."

Getting to work with Alec would ease the pain of having to clean a nasty bathroom. It was a dream come true.

Buy Love is Murder on Amazon

https://www.amazon.com/gp/product/B06VT4WZD3

If you'd like updates on the newest books I'm writing, follow me on Amazon and Facebook:

https://www.facebook.com/
Kathleen-Suzette-Kate-Bell-authors-759206390932120/

https://www.amazon.com/Kathleen-Suzette/e/
B07B7D2S4W/ref=dp_byline_cont_pop_ebooks_1

Made in the USA
Coppell, TX
17 October 2023

22989813R00100